"When I read Robert Fish's stories, I hear my own higher self speaking to me, reminding me of life's true priorities and of how to keep paying attention to them. Fish has the ability to make even the tiniest of life's incidents into a warm, informative story. He shares the yearnings and learnings of his own heart freely; his stories are a generous outpouring, both provocative and inspiring.

"*The Woman Who Walked to Paradise* is like a little treasure box to carry around. Whenever you peek inside (read a story), a gentle thought or image floats out, to lighten up your day and move you just a bit closer to your true self."

— Susan Page, Author of *How One of You Can Bring the Two of You Together*

"Fish's stories combine timeless wisdom with wry humor and everyman humility. A hit!"

— Mississippi author Ernest Herndon

"There's something refreshing about the author of a self-help book offering the following sage advice for conquering procrastination: 'Allow guilt to consume you.' ...

"Fish has written a disarming collection of auto-biographical sketches and folktales that share a common thread of fragile humanness. 'Just because I teach stress reduction,' Fish confides to us, 'I wouldn't want you to get the idea that I always have it together.' The author's self-effacing candor sets his book apart from the inspirational literature by Schwarzenegger-like champions of confidence-building. ...

"Storytelling—as an art form and a motivational tool—is central to Fish's way of looking at the world. He believes that by expressing our fears honestly, we can learn to rewrite the way in which we narrate our lives. ...

"The insights steer clear of trendy psychobabble or easy palliatives. Worth the price of admission are the autobiographical sketches, which are first-rate."

—Bob Wake, author of *Caffeine & Other Stories*

The Woman Who Walked To Paradise

Stories for Coping in a Chaotic World

by Robert Stevens Fish, Ph.D.

FISH TALES  PRESS

Published by Fish Tales Press
1140 Newport Avenue
San Jose, CA 95125-3329

Printed in cooperation with Patchwork Press at 1-800-738-6721.

Printed in the United States of America

Publisher's Cataloging-in-Publication
(Provided by Quality Books, Inc.)

Fish, Robert Stevens.
    The woman who walked to paradise : stories for coping
in a chaotic world / by Robert Stevens Fish. -- 1st ed.

    p. cm.
    Includes bibliographical references.
    ISBN: 1-892193-04-3
    1. Stress (Psychology) 2. Conduct of life.
3. Spirituality. I. Title.

    BF575.S75F57 2000   155.9'042
                               QBI00-901066

I wish to thank the copyright holders for permission to quote from the following sources:

From *The Artist's Way* by Julia Cameron, copyright © 1992 by Julia Cameron. Used by permission of Jeremy P. Tarcher, a Division of Penguin Putnam Inc.

Archy and Mehitabel, by Don Marquis, pu-http://www.lanebryant.com/corporate/gift_cert/coupon.cfm?ID=58296-8blished by Doubleday & Company, Inc. Reprinted by permission.

"Healing Power, McGwire Overcame Injuries," by Bud Geracie, September 4, 1999. Copyright © 1999 San Jose Mercury News. All rights reserved. Reproduced with permission. Use of this material does not imply endorsement of the San Jose Mercury News.

Wherever You Go, There You Are, by Jon Kabat-Zinn, copyright © 1994, published by Hyperion Books. Reprinted by permission.

Copyright © 1996, by Win Wenger and Richard Poel, from the book *The Einstein Factor*, Prima Publishing, Roseville, CA. Buy or order at bookstores or call (800) 632-8676 or contact Prima at www.primapublishing.com.

Get What You Want, by Patricia Fripp, copyright © 1998 Patricia Fripp, published by Executive Books. For more information contact (800) 634-3035, email PFripp@aol.com, or http://www.fripp.com.

The Teaching of Buddha, published by Bukkyo Dendo Kyokai, Tokyo, copyright © 1966 Bukkyo Dendo Kyokai.

Cover Design: Robert Regis Dvorák
Printed by: DeHart's Printing Services Corporation

If most of us remain ignorant of ourselves, it is because self-knowledge is painful and we prefer the pleasure of illusion.

— Aldous Huxley

To my spiritual mentors—
Stan and Susan Burnett-Hampson, Sonika
Tinker, Mary-Wayne Bush, Patricia
WhiteBuffalo, and Kent Bond.
Namaste

PREFACE

In the fall of 1996 I was looking for a way to stay in touch with the participants in my stress management workshops. I knew that without reminders and encouragement, most people would revert to their former stressful behaviors.

I started writing a weekly "Stress Tip." I sent it out by email on Sunday evening so people could read it on Monday morning (typically the most stressful day of the week).

I wanted to make the essays personal, as though I were speaking directly to the reader. I revealed my own struggles with stress.

Some people asked me to stop sending them the essays. Many others forwarded them to friends and associates who then asked me to add them to the mailing list. The list has grown in three years from ten to over 700.

Over time, the essays began to deal with stress more indirectly, so I changed the name to "View From the Fishbowl." I'm still writing them, and this book is a collection of the best of those essays.

My hope is that you'll find them helpful, encouraging, funny, soothing, even inspiring. I intend them to be gentle reminders that life is an amazing, incredible experience. We are meant to live fully, with love and enthusiasm. Sometimes we forget this. We knew it when we were very young.

Take a deep breath. Enjoy the moment.

Robert Stevens Fish
San Jose, California

ACKNOWLEDGMENTS

A s with almost all projects, this book is the result of many hands.

Special thanks go to:

Diana Bonet, for her editing and guidance.

Sybil Rossiter, my assistant, for designing the book layout and for keeping me laughing during the dark hours.

Linda Lenore, Jim Horan, Amy Berger, and Barry Evans, who have written their own books and lit the path for me.

Sandy Jones, for proofing the manuscript with her keen eye.

Susan Sparrow, who could see the big picture and the small details simultaneously.

Rebecca Morgan, my wife, for her early encouragement.

And to all those who have been faithful readers of the email "View From the Fishbowl" columns over the last three years.

HOW TO CONTACT THE AUTHOR

Robert Stevens Fish, Ph.D., is a stress management expert and a professional storyteller. He provides talks, workshops and consulting services for organizations and businesses nationwide. Requests for information about these services, as well as inquiries about his avaliability for speeches and workshops, should be directed to him at the address below. To receive Robert's weekly articles by email, sign up on his website. You're encouraged to write to Robert with comments or your stories of coping in a chaotic world.

Robert Stevens Fish
Fish Tales Press
1440 Newport Avenue
San Jose, CA 95125
(408) 998-7978
1-877-88DRFISH (toll free)
Fax: (408) 998-1742
Email: robertfish@aol.com
Web site: www.robertfish.com

TABLE OF CONTENTS

1: HEALTH

The Wake-up Call

Every day is a good day.
—Yun-men

As a stress management coach and workshop leader, I've worked hard to be the best in my field. But I have to admit that I'd focused my attention primarily on the mental aspects of stress reduction. In terms of the body, I know a fair amount about exercise and diet, but that's about it. I was never interested much in healing the body, perhaps because I'd been blessed with good health. So, like many people, I took my health for granted.

Recently I had an opportunity to become more knowledgeable about health and healing. In the spring of 1998, I went in for a colonoscopy, a viewing of the interior of the colon. The doctor found two tiny polyps that he clipped out. No problem. Then he found a third one, larger, hidden in a fold, impossible to clip. He nipped a corner off for a biopsy. The report came back: pre-cancerous, meaning it's not malignant now but probably will be within a year or so.

The doctor's advice: surgery! Have ten to twelve inches of the colon removed to get rid of the polyp. I went to my General Practitioner. He said the same. I worried that it was major surgery.

"No, it's not," the GP said. "Open heart surgery, that's major. Brain surgery, that's major. This is not a big deal." He was starting to sound like Stanley in the movie *Wag the Dog*: "This is nothing!"

Okay, I thought, I don't like it, but okay. I had grown up in a family that never challenged the doctor. The doctor was the ultimate authority.

So I dutifully made an appointment with the surgeon who would do the deed. I asked him about the operation that was not a big deal.

"It's a three hour procedure." (Why do they always call it a procedure?) "You'll be in the hospital for a week, out of commission for three, and you won't be back to normal for eight weeks." (This is not a big deal?)

"I should also mention that there's always the slight risk of a heart attack or stroke on the operating table," (Oh?) "as well as chance of an infection afterward. But we'll be able to treat that with antibiotics." (Well, thank goodness for that..)

"Your polyp is in a tricky place. There are a lot of nerves behind that section. So there's also a small risk of permanent impotence or damage to the prostate gland. I operate on Fridays. I'm going on vacation for a few days so I can't take you this Friday, but how about a week from now? We can set it up today."

I was in shock. Not a big deal? Not a big deal? THIS WAS A VERY BIG DEAL!

I staggered out of the surgeon's office, confused and upset. I didn't like this at all.

What was I going to do?

The following week, I mentioned my concerns to a friend who suggested I look into alternative healing. And the light bulb went on. I remembered reading about cases where people actually made tumors disappear through holistic health practices.

I made a deal with my GP. I would spend the next four months attempting to heal myself using alternative methods. Then I would go back in for another colonoscopy. If the polyp wasn't any smaller, I would go in for the surgery. But, if I was able to reduce it . . . .

So I began an incredible journey in an attempt to heal my body and escape the scalpel. The polyp was a wake-up call. The message was that I'm not immortal and that my life needed more balance *right now*, not next month or next year. I'm grateful for the polyp; without it, I wouldn't be on this journey toward better health, a stronger mind, and deeper spiritual practices. I feel as though I have begun to awaken, and since wakefulness is my major goal in life, how can I be ungrateful?

For a healthier body, I am utilizing:
- vitamin therapy
- enzyme therapy
- acupuncture with a doctor of oriental medicine
- network chiropractic
- colon cleansings
- yoga
- vegetarianism
- Dr. Kenneth Cooper's antioxidant regimen of exercise and vitamins
- reflexology

To use my mind as a partner in this journey, I am reading such books as:
- Siegel, Bernie. *Love, Medicine & Miracles*
- Myss, Caroline. *Why People Don't Heal and How They Can*
- Trowbridge, Bob. *The Hidden Meaning of Illness*
- Ornish, Dean. *Love & Survival*

- Talbot, Michael. *The Holographic Universe*
- Kaufman, Barry Neil. *Happiness is a Choice*

I'll be adding books by Deepak Chopra, Louise Hay, Gerald Jampolsky, Robert Ornstein, and others.

I'm also practicing:

- meditation
- guided imagery
- self-hypnosis and hypnotherapy
- surfacing unresolved issues

For the spirit, I am going on a silent prayer retreat in a few weeks, and talking to people, including my counselor/therapist, about life as a spiritual journey.

Why am I sharing all of this with you? Undoubtedly, it's more than you ever wanted to know. I'm sharing it because we're all on the same path, trying to live our lives as best we can, striving to be healthy and happy and to contribute to a better world. If we can learn from each other's experiences, so much the better. Take whatever makes sense, and leave the rest.

Also, if you're over fifty, get a colonoscopy. It's a lot better to find a polyp than it is to find a tumor. (Ask Darryl Strawberry, the New York Yankees' baseball player who had a procedure for a walnut-size tumor in his colon. Incredibly, he was only thirty-six at the time.)

Polyps I Have Loved
Nine months later

Last week I went in for another colonoscopy.

The doctor located Mr. Polyp. "It doesn't look as angry as it did earlier, but it's still there. You have three options: I could try to snip it out again, you could go in for surgery, or you could do nothing." I chose door number one. "Good, that was my choice, too," he said.

He worked for awhile, then said, "We're getting it."

And he did. All of it. Then he said an interesting thing: "I don't know what changed from the last time I tried to snare this thing, but this time it presented itself to me."

I'm sure there's a biological explanation for the change: given a lifetime of neglect and abuse, my colon was no doubt stressed, perhaps oddly twisted. After nine months of various alternative healing measures, the colon may have returned to a more normal shape, allowing the doctor to snare the polyp.

There's also a metaphysical explanation that I accept: the polyp came into my body to wake me up, to shock me into reevaluating what's important in my life, and to get me on a healthier path of mind, body, and spirit. It had achieved its goal, so there was no more need to stick around. It could go.

In terms of changes to my body: I am now a vegetarian and loving it; I take vitamin supplements (some of the vitamins are part of an antioxidant regimen); I walk briskly four to five times a week for two-and-a-half miles; I go to yoga classes as often as I can (I had begun yoga six months before the discovery of the polyp); I have colon hydrotherapy treatments every three weeks.

On the mental front, I've been a student of meditation for some time. I believe strongly in its value, though I often have to struggle to sit down and practice it. (I know— if it's a struggle, I'm not approaching it correctly; but if I don't struggle I can go weeks without doing it at all.) I'm now committed to dream analysis, which has been quite valuable to me, as has mental imagery in various forms. I have hypnotherapy sessions every now and then. (I practice hypnosis on my own, too.) I have read about two dozen books and attended many workshops. I haven't added up how much money I've spent on all these activities, but I've heard you can't put a price on good health. Whatever I've spent, it was cheaper than having an operation that cuts out a foot of my colon and puts me in danger of impotence, prostate damage, infection, and even death.

On the spiritual side, I've increased my awareness of a higher power and have become a believer in the power of prayer. I've attended workshops to increase my intuition and spiritual awareness. I've begun to explore the healing arts, both as a client (I've seen a number of medical intuitives, with outstanding results) and as a student. I've become more grateful, less judgmental, and more accepting of life in general. I am happier; I appreciate the beauty of blue skies and gray skies and rainy skies and night skies. Life is good, and it's getting better all the time.

I am truly grateful for the polyp's arrival in my life. Without it, I would be less aware, less healthy, less awake than I am today.

If we're lucky, we don't have to have a threat to health and life to wake up.

Good-bye, Mr. Polyp. And thank you.

2: ANGER

Flame-O-Grams

Anger is the emotion preeminently serviceable for the display of power.

— Walter B. Cannon

Short temper is a loss of face.

— fortune cookie

Some time ago, I received an interesting series of emails. Perhaps you got them too—they went out to a lot of people.

The first one began with a long list of everyone who had received the email. I had to scroll down through a *lot* of addresses to get to the message. The message was about a little girl who was dying of cancer and had written a poem about how we should live life more fully. The writer then asked us to forward this email to all of our friends, because "for every person you send it to, The American Cancer Society will donate three cents per name to [the girl's] treatment and recovery plan."

A second email arrived a day later. It was a response to the first. The writer went into a tirade about how idiotic the first writer was, what a colossal waste of time the email was, and what maudlin and sentimental claptrap the whole thing was. He pointed out that the Cancer Society would have no way of knowing how many people had received the email, further proof of the stupidity of the writer. I could almost feel the anger surging through my screen. He sent this to everyone who had received the first email. A lot of people.

Finally, a day or two later, a third email arrived. It was from the angry man again. It was an apology. He said he had been tired, under a lot of pressure, and he had read the letter at a bad time and snapped. He admitted to overreacting.

Here was an example of unmanaged stress. I wonder if that guy has a habit of bad days like that. If so, he risks damage to his relationships, to his ability to do his job well, and to his health.

Like traffic jams and bad drivers, unwanted email is becoming a part of our cyberlives. Some of the worst are the ads for pornography. At first it was easy to spot them, with subjects like "Looking for a good time?" and "I just turned eighteen and I'm ready."

But they're getting more clever. Now the subject line says things like, "I forgot to tell you," "I'm sorry," (appropriate for our hotheaded friend), "One more thing," and my personal favorite, "Did you receive our check?"

Deleting these messages without opening them takes a little time. Opening them first takes more time.

I used to get irritated myself, until I got that it's like commute traffic—it's not going to go away.

My new attitude toward junk email is that it's a signal for a time out—I take a few deep breaths to clear my mind and relax for however long it takes to clear the screen. I've got an old clunker, so it can take as long as five seconds to delete an email. Fine, that's a five second break. I close my eyes and take two slow deep breaths.

Our friend might argue that he's too busy to take a time out. My response to him is that he would be more centered and relaxed and able to make better decisions over the next thirty minutes if he did. If we think we can't spare a few seconds, we're not delegating enough to others.

There's a parallel here to the trend in road rage, that of losing our patience and our tempers at what we perceive to be the stupidity of other people and then doing even more stupid things to exact revenge or to vent our emotions. The words we let loose in a Flame-O-Gram go careening down the internet like a two-ton pickup crossing the median. Watch out.

Anger—You Got a Problem With That?

A reader wrote to me about anger:

> I'm in favor of anger. . . . I'm not going with any flow. I run the risk of pissing people off and hurting relationships, I know. Overall, I try to use judgment—but I've seen what happens to people who stuff it down. I'd rather bust a gut being pissed than try to be mellow. I remember a great cartoon that showed a grave with a mound of dirt and a headstone. Sticking up through the ground was a hand, giving the finger. Now that's my kind of guy.

This reader, let's call him Richard, makes a valid point: suppressing anger is about as dangerous to our health as blowing up. Both options have been shown, in study after study, to raise blood pressure and contribute to coronary heart disease.

So we're damned if we do and damned if we don't. Is there a way out of this anger trap? Richard makes it seem as though venting or stuffing are the only two options available. Is there another option?

Yes, but first, you need to *want* to be less angry. If you don't think the damage you do to your health and relationships outweighs the satisfaction you get from your outbursts, you won't change. Period. I'm struck by how many angry people are proud of their anger. It's like a badge of honor.

Assuming you want to change, one next step is to accept that the source of your anger isn't out there. It's your interpretation of what's *happening* out there, it's your response to your own thoughts. This is a tough one to accept in light of all the stupidity and greed that needs fixing and the perpetrators who need punishing. I'm not suggesting that wrongs don't need to be righted. But we can still be a social activist, for example, and not destroy our bodies with anger as we undo the evildoers.

Another step is to decide what's worth our anger and what isn't. Traffic's a good example. In the Bay Area, heavy traffic is a given. It's almost impossible to avoid. It's like the air; it's all around us, all the time. Yet, lots of people go berserk out on the highways as though they're surprised to see all the cars and all the bad drivers. These people can get angry ten times a week just driving to and from work. What's wrong with this picture?

Anger is a choice, as happiness is a choice. A tough choice sometimes, but a choice nevertheless.

So if you've decided you want to be less angry, and you've decided some things aren't worth your anger (e.g., traffic), the next step is to alert your monitor, your internal observer, as you approach the situation that triggers the anger. Coach yourself: "Heads up now. You don't have to get angry this time. Just this one time, you can stay calm."

Start with the easy ones. Celebrate your wins. Forgive yourself for slips. If you're interested in reducing your anger, I recommend the book *Anger Kills*, by Redford and Virginia Williams.

My problem with the guy who's sticking his hand up out of his grave, giving the world the finger for the last time, is that he probably died at fifty of a heart attack.

Anger, One Letter Short of Danger

I heard from Richard again, who, as you know, takes a position in favor of anger. He wrote, "That unconflicted, clear connection with anger will help all of us set limits and tell the world where the boundaries are."

He's right. Anger does that. At the same time, we have other ways to "set limits and tell the world where our boundaries are" that don't include the harmful components (to self and others) of anger.

The mail I received demonstrates that we all have a story to tell about anger. Here's one story from a reader:

> I had an angry father. He maintained that it was good to get things off his chest and out in the open. Well, it may have been good for him. He lived to ninety, but he made life not so good for his family. Part of his legacy to his children was that anger. Not that I express anger in the rageful way that he did, but I think that my anger response was affected by his behavior—I get angry at things I really don't want to get angry at.

Here, the father's anger didn't result in a heart attack or stroke, but it did result in damage to the family, to the people he presumably loved the most.

My wife and I come from families that expressed anger in different ways. Rebecca's parents had explosive bouts of anger: yelling, screaming, slamming doors, threats of violence, throwing clothes onto the lawn. She made up her mind at an early age that she would be different.

I grew up in a house that was just the opposite: my mother used silence as a weapon when she was angry. She withdrew. She wouldn't talk, except in clipped sentences or requests. Her simmering silence could go on for days.

In my house, the outward expression of anger was right up there with sex and death—a taboo. I remember my mother saying to me, angrily, "Don't you get mad at me, young man," or "You don't have any reason to be angry," or "Don't be so sensitive." Those remarks, of course, made me even angrier.

The result was the same for both Rebecca and me. We grew up fearing anger, suppressing our anger—not being comfortable with either our own or someone else's. Is it any surprise that we chose each other? We couldn't have lived with someone who had an explosive or smoldering temper. It would have been too much like home. For some years, however, we created our own problems by pretending we weren't angry. Working with a counselor disabused us of that belief.

Angry people don't really understand the damage they create around them, either at work or at home. I have seen adults shake and cry from angry outbursts directed at them by coworkers and bosses. "Those people just need to be more thick-skinned," the angry boss might say, in defense of his outburst. It is, of course, not that simple.

William C. Menninger, M.D., has published a list called "The Criteria of Emotional Maturity." On the list he includes, "The capacity to sublimate, to direct one's instinctive hostile energy into creative and constructive outlets." I like that.

At the same time that I like the idea, I struggle with

it. How do I find the healthiest way to express anger so that I'm free of it, and so that my relationship with the person I was angry at is stronger as a result?

There are many different approaches, and we've all got to find our own road.

Here's a good exercise to do with a group of friends. Everyone take a turn answering this question: how was anger expressed in your home when you were growing up? That ought to stir the pot a little.

Anger and More Anger

Here are some readers' comments on anger. From Chris:

In Jerry Jampolsky's little book, *Goodbye to Guilt*, he summarizes the radical and provocative "A Course in Miracles" in about 12 short lessons. One of my favorites right now is "I am not angry for the reason I think." You can also substitute "upset," "afraid," "depressed" and so on for "angry."

Right now I am practicing this awareness with my life partner, Anna.

She was getting on my nerves with her constant chatter and especially the parts where she wants me to participate by answering the questions, "Why? Don't you agree?"

So I was yelling at her about something. Yelling. Can't remember what. I think it was about her criticizing a letter that I helped her (at her insistence) to write.

She just looked at me and said, "You are yelling at me because you are mad at yourself or something else." Bingo! Zingo!

Luckily I had some practice at this sort of thing, so that I could instantly recognize the truth of what she said and even what I was really angry at. Because ten years ago I would have become enraged if someone said that to me and bombarded them with furious insults that they would probably never forget. Bombardment is one of my talents that I have pretty much given up now.

The central problem with anger is what the proponents of macho bellowing don't want to see. Anger is most often wrongly displayed toward the weak and innocent, such as children, or strangers who have to provide customer service on the telephone. That is what I was doing to Anna.

The other thing wrong with expressing anger in the traditional modes is that it helps us to hide from our own insight about what the hell it is we need to get a grip on. That is also what I was doing so that I would not have to admit that I was furious with myself for not firing State Farm Insurance before my auto policy anniversary date.

As the insurance tizzy later turned out, State Farm really was giving me the best rate I could get in Dallas, and so I was angry FOR NOTHING AT ALL in the long run. But I had yelled at someone younger, smaller, and less able to deal with business than I am.

I am so glad that you were writing about anger. I love the way it makes people mad to criticize anger. I love the way people get savage and unforgiving when you tell them that forgiveness is not optional.

Here's a letter from Alan:

Anger is of itself a healthy, normal response. Without an ability to become angry and sustain anger, we would be useless creatures and completely defenseless. Without it, men especially would be unable to sustain much in the way of outward accomplishment.

That said, simply because one feels angry does not mean that the anger MUST be expressed in destructive ways. As human beings we have that moment of choice when we realize a feeling and get to decide what our expression will be, which is what becoming an adult is about.

I too grew up in a mixed home. My father was so busy being reasonable and rational that he would never admit that he was angry. My mother, on the other hand, spent her life as an angry woman. She took out her anger by flying off at the kids, complete with verbal and physical violence.

As the father of a very willful three year old, it is my constant task to remain in balance. I need to let him know that I am angry when he pushes me over the line without taking out my frustration and anger on his little psyche (or his little body). Hopefully, he will learn that he does not have to be owned by his anger—and that he doesn't have to pretend that his anger isn't there.

From Carla:

I tried to stay out of this, but the phrase below nailed me and I couldn't let it go: "I think angry people don't really understand the damage they create around them." I have lived with both my family of origin and my current family (now does that sound like someone who has been in therapy for eight years or not?). Some died before I could work out all of the problems that their anger caused me, but some are still around for me to get revenge (not really). However, when I discuss what their angry outbursts do to me and others, they have a hard time understanding. Since they can get angry and just blow it off, they think I can do the same. Tain't so! But usually the folks who don't get this probably want to set boundaries and get some kind of gratification from controlling others through anger and ridicule.

Here's a note from Brian:

> The best thing I ever heard about anger is that it's a power trip. We most often express anger around people when we know we can get away with it.
>
> My own observation is that I'm never really angry at the thing I'm angry at. For example, when I'm pissed at someone on the road, it's usually because I'm late and feel they're slowing me down. My worst and angriest moments are when I'm late and rushing to try to make up time—a tack I'm outgrowing slowly.
>
> The other reason I get mad on the road (or elsewhere) is that someone does something so utterly unpredictable and dumb that it actually scares me—though I usually express this as anger (i.e., "dumb____!!").

And from Arnold:

> I couldn't help but think of all the spam and nasty messages that I have received over the years. I think you have to roll with the spam. I will delete mail without reading it, if I am pretty sure that it is spam. However, I find myself sometimes chuckling at the one that gets through as the result of a creative hook that I fell for.
>
> It took me awhile to learn how to handle

flame-o-grams or flamers, as I call them. As most
people do, I first experienced them at work. As a
sender or respondent, my first inclination was to
fire something off in a reflexive (screw you too)
manner. It hit me one day while sailing on the Bay
that I had misconstrued the content of a message
and found myself wishing that I had not pressed
the send icon on Friday. Since then, I have tried
not to write something hot. If I think it is, I set it
aside for a day or so and then go back to it. You
can't believe the number of self-initiated email
messages or pending responses that I have
deleted. More importantly, as I have developed
my spiritual practice, I have found myself not
responding in kind. I typically walk down the
hallway or pick up the phone.

I have found that the Buddha of Compassion
has helped me to develop compassion for what is
going on out there—whether it's everyday space
or cyberspace.

Barbara sent in these root sources of the word
"anger" and a quotation from Julia Cameron:

ANGER: Latin—*angustus*, narrow; *angustia*,
tightness; *angre*, to strangle. Greek—*anchein*, to
squeeze; *anchone*, a strangling. German—*angst*,
fear.

From *The Artist's Way*, by Julia Cameron:

Anger is fuel. We feel it and we want to do
something. Hit someone, break something, throw
a fit, smash a fist into the wall, tell those bastards.
But we are nice people, and what we do with our

anger is stuff it, deny it, bury it, block it, hide it, lie about it, medicate it, muffle it, ignore it. We do everything but listen to it.

Anger is meant to be listened to. Anger is a voice, a shout, a plea, a demand. Anger is meant to be respected. Why? Because anger is a map. Anger points the way. Anger is meant to be acted upon. It is not meant to be acted out.

When we feel anger, we are often very angry that we feel anger. It tells us that old life is dying. It tells us we are being reborn, and birthing hurts. The hurt makes us angry.

Sloth, apathy, and despair are the enemy. Anger is not. Anger is our friend. Not a nice friend. Not a gentle friend. But a very, very loyal friend.

Enough on anger. It's starting to tick me off.

Driving Demons

J ust because I teach stress reduction, I wouldn't want you to get the idea that I always have it together. Here's a tale of one of my driving demons.

I turn onto the entrance ramp to Interstate 280 in San Jose. It's a long, uphill ramp, maybe a hundred yards or so. It begins as two lanes, then narrows to one lane at the crest of the ramp where it enters 280.

My acceleration is slow to moderate as I go up the ramp. Okay, to tell the truth, my car is old and sluggish. If I had a Corvette, I would approach the ramp a bit more energetically. As it is, I drive in the right hand lane.

Half-way up the ramp, I look in the rear-view mirror. Here he comes. His car is back at the entrance to the on-ramp, and I can tell by his acceleration that he's already planning to pass me.

He barrels up the ramp. Let him pass, let him pass, I say to myself, but I push harder on the gas pedal. Damn it, it's not fair. He shouldn't get ahead of me. It's not right.

Here he comes, squeezing past me as the two lanes become one. He doesn't look at me. He doesn't seem to care how close our cars are.

I look over. It's a young guy, a kid. Wearing a baseball cap. Backward. I get angry. I don't want to, but I give in to it. It feels good to give in to it.

I stomp on the gas and down shift for more oomph. It's too little, too late. We're on the interstate, he has careened over three lanes into the fast lane. He disappears, leaving me with raised blood-pressure and anger, anger, anger.

That scenario recurred at least twice a week.

I used to live a block away from the on-ramp. I had to use it daily. It was my crucible. I would be tested at 7 A.M. every day for my ability to stay calm. I failed frequently. Far too often.

Once I got so angry I tried to overtake the evildoer, driving so dangerously that when I finally got hold of myself and slowed down, a number of drivers honked and shook their fists or middle fingers at me as they passed. I was humiliated. I might have killed someone, myself included.

Another time, a car pulled onto the on-ramp ahead of me and did something I took offense to. I was so angry that I tailgated him for a short while, then downshifted into second, (I would have gone to first if I'd had to, because this guy was not going to get away with whatever it was he had done) and pulled into the left lane to pass him before we reached the moment of truth where two lanes became one.

As I passed this creep, I glared over at him. He was an older man, maybe in his sixties, robust, not feeble or anything, with a huge white beard and strong, penetrating eyes. He had a softness about his face, and I had two immediate images: Santa Claus and an actor in a Biblical epic.

All the fire went out of me. I felt small, insignificant, stupid. I slowed down and let him go ahead.

Luckily, I moved out of that neighborhood and was able to avoid the "on-ramp from hell" from then on.

A year or so later, I found myself back in the neighborhood. I wanted to drive by the old house. It looked about the same. And there was the on-ramp. To avoid it, I would have to go four blocks out of my way. Oh what the heck, I thought. That's all behind me now, just a bad memory.

I turned onto the ramp into the right-hand lane, with nice smooth acceleration (I still had my old, slow car.) Everything was good. Then I looked in the rear-view mirror. Oh no. Here he was again, gunning it.

He's going to do it, going to scrape by me again as the lanes merge, I think. I couldn't get enough acceleration in time to stay ahead. His car blasted past me, and I felt the old anger coming back in spite of all my intentions. I looked over.

It was a woman. Then my male ego kicked in. I turned purple. I couldn't stand it. It was as though nothing had changed.

It was like going home after being away for twenty years and your mother pushes your old buttons with that old, familiar tone of voice. You're ten years old in an instant and reacting in the same old immature way.

Finally I saw the irony in the situation and let go of the anger. But I had failed the test once again.

I don't know why that particular situation draws out such competitiveness in me, but it does. And I have to admit that I am powerless over it.

So what's the lesson? Know specifically what pushes your buttons. Be alert to your negative emotional responses when you go into those situations. Try to head it off. Don't let emotions get the upper hand. If your coping strategies don't work, try avoiding the situation. Life's too short to waste it on fighting with our driving demons.

"The Samurai and the Monk"
A Zen Folktale

A samurai came to visit an old Zen monk. "I want you to teach me of heaven and hell," the warrior demanded.

The little monk looked the samurai up and down, squinting his eyes.

"Well?" the samurai barked impatiently.

The monk tilted his head. "Teach you of heaven and hell? Why should I teach you anything? Look at you. You're filthy. Your sword is rusty. Your hands are dirty. You've obviously been out of work for some time. And with good reason, I would say. Go away."

The samurai blew up. No one spoke to him in that manner and lived. With a growl, he drew his sword and lifted it over his head to slice the monk in half.

In the instant before the sword began its downward path, the monk pointed up to him and said, "That's hell."

The samurai hesitated . . . and understood what the monk meant. At the same time, he realized that the monk had been willing to risk his own life to teach him this lesson. He was struck with the bravery of the little man.

He lowered his sword and bowed to the monk.

"And that," the monk said, pointing to him again, "is heaven."

3: ATTITUDE

"Is That So?"
A Zen Folktale

There's a Zen story about a teenage girl who got pregnant. She was frightened, so when her parents asked her who the father was, she lied and said it was the old Zen monk down the road.

When the baby was born, the angry parents went to the monk's little cottage and banged on his door. When the monk answered, the father said, "This baby is yours," and held it out to him.

The monk said, "Is that so?" and took the baby.

Over the next few years, the monk raised the child with as much concern and tenderness and love as if it had been his own.

Meanwhile, the teenage girl was overcome by remorse and told her parents the truth, that the father was her boyfriend.

The parents, in righteous indignation, marched back to the monk's home and pounded on the door again. When the monk appeared, the angry father said, "The child is not yours. We want it back."

The monk said, "Is that so?" and gave them the child.

Now before you read any further, take a moment to assess your reactions to the story.

Is it about a passive old man who won't or can't stand up for his rights? What's wrong with him? Why did he let the parents get away with it? Didn't he have a backbone? That can't be good for the child.

To me, this story is about acceptance and non-judgment. Aren't we all quick to get upset and angry when our rights have been violated in some way? Don't we all have boundaries beyond which interlopers tread at great peril? We're pretty clear about what's right and what's wrong where we're involved, and we will howl if we feel wronged. (That explains in part why there are so many lawyers making a good living.)

One of the major ways we can relieve our stress is to back off from some of the endless judgments we make of others. The most challenging to give up are the judgments we make when we've been wronged.

Still, you may be thinking, that story is beyond the fringe; it's so far out as to be silly, stupid. Nobody would or could be that unattached to things. No one would want to be.

Maybe not. Certainly I don't know anyone capable of being that unattached, including me. Especially me.

So what's the point?

I think the story holds out an ideal, an image of perfection that we will never attain in this life but that we might aspire to. Whatever else you may think of the monk, he's not stressed. He lives in serenity. Nothing bothers him, not even an assault like the one described. That's worth aspiring to.

Think back on your reactions. Did you get angry at the monk? Did you quickly dismiss him as foolish or stupid or worse?

So the next time some jerk cuts you off on the highway, instead of yelling "#@%&**#@!!," think "Is that so?"

Lou the Barber

My barber, Lou, is quite a storyteller. But one he told recently topped them all. He told me why he'd been out of his shop for three months.

Lou loves motorcycles. He bought a Harley last year. He parked it outside the shop. It was a work of art, all black and chrome.

One day he was driving slowly through a parking lot when a car backed out in front of him. He laid the bike down to avoid hitting the car, but his foot caught in a collapsing foot pedal. His leg, from knee to ankle, was twisted like a wet shirt, and the bones were shattered in a dozen places.

The doctors set his leg with pins, screws, pipes and rods. Then, while he was in surgery, a blood clot lodged in his lungs. If he hadn't been in a hospital, he would have died.

There's more, but I'll spare you the details.

Recently I went in for a haircut. Lou was back. He was hopping around with a cane and a high-tech cast. He sat on a stool to cut hair.

And he was laughing. Without a word of complaint or self-pity. He didn't act as if he'd been given a bum deal. He told this story as he tells all of his stories: with humor and zest. He reminds me of Zorba the Greek— whatever cards he's dealt, he plays with passion and energy.

I was struck by how, in the six or seven years I've gone to Lou's place for haircuts, he has consistently maintained an upbeat, positive attitude.

Two years ago he became a part-time cop. "It was something I'd always wanted to do," he said. First there were the stories of struggling to get through the police academy. Then there were the on-the-beat stories.

Here I heard a tinge of sadness behind his bright, boisterous exterior. Some of the things he had to do bothered him. One day, he quit.

"I didn't like what I was becoming. It wasn't worth it," he said, shrugging. He had busted his butt to fulfill a dream of becoming a cop, then he walked away without a regret. The guy is incredible.

Lucky for me, Lou gives a great haircut, so I don't have to put up with bad hair to get my monthly fix of his homespun philosophy.

There is one little detail that bugs Lou about his accident. The elderly woman who backed out in front of him got out of her car, went over to where he was pinned under his motorcycle, asked how he was, said she'd go for help, drove away, and never returned. No one saw her license plate number.

"I'm looking for her," he said. "She was driving a white Bonneville." Lou used to be a boxer. For her sake, I hope the old lady sold her car. Or at least had it painted.

"Perfect Joy"
A Story of St. Francis

St. Francis' preferred method of transportation was walking. He walked everywhere. For him, walking was a spiritual practice. His companion was often Leo, a young, devoted, and good-natured brother in Francis' order.

On one trip, the two were returning to the friary from Perugia on a cold, wet, wintry afternoon. As they walked, Leo, in spite of himself, lamented that he was soaked through, cold, tired, and hungry.

Francis asked him if he knew what perfect joy was.

"No, Father Francis, I do not," Leo muttered, hunching his shoulders against the wind and freezing rain.

Francis said, "If we brothers had all the knowledge in the world and were able to dispense it to the betterment of mankind, would that be perfect joy?"

Before Leo could answer, Francis barked, "No, it would not."

They continued to walk along the rocky road in silence. Then Francis said, "Brother Leo, if we brothers could heal every disease, if we could make the blind see and make the deaf to hear, if we could raise the dead, would that be perfect joy? No. No, it would not."

More silence. Leo squinted into the rain, as confused as he was tired.

"Brother Leo, if we brothers were able to preach so that every person who heard us found grace in God's love, if we were able to convert everyone on earth, would that be perfect joy?"

By this time, although Leo thought that yes, that would be perfect joy, he knew better than to say anything.

"No, it wouldn't," roared Francis. "Mark it well, it would not be."

More silence. They walked for miles. Leo's curiosity was killing him.

"Father Francis, for the love of God, tell me what perfect joy is."

Francis shook the rain from his face and smiled at Leo.

"Ah, Brother Leo, little lamb of God, listen carefully. We are only a few miles away from Portiuncula, our beloved friary. Notice that the temperature is falling. The rain is turning to sleet. When we arrive it will be dark, too. If we knock loudly on the door, should Brother Porter answer, who is old and half-blind, and he should ask us, 'Who are you?' we would say, 'It is Francis and Leo, let us in.' And Brother Porter might say 'You are liars and thieves. Francis is not expected until tomorrow. Go away.' And he would slam the door in our face. That, Brother Leo, is perfect joy."

"But, but, holy father," Leo began. Francis interrupted him.

"And so, after waiting a time, beating our arms and legs to create some warmth against the freezing rain, we pound again on the door, begging to be let in. This time Brother Porter comes to the second floor window and yells at us, 'Be gone, you vermin, do not make me angry,' and he throws a pail of greasy kitchen water on us. It freezes to our skin. That, Brother Leo, is perfect joy."

Leo stared at Francis in disbelief. He even forgot how miserable he was.

"So we wait, Brother Leo, until we can stand it no longer, and we knock again, weeping, crying out to please, for the love of God, let us in, even if it's to sleep in the kitchen hallway, and Brother Porter rushes out with a knobby stick, yelling 'All right, I'll teach you two murderers a lesson,' and he beats us with the stick and throws us into the muddy, icy ditch. Then he bolts the door shut and goes off to bed. That," Francis shouted triumphantly, "is perfect joy!"

Leo was beside himself. "Please . . . how . . . .?"

"Brother Leo, listen to me well. It is easy to find joy in a beautiful day, a good meal, comfortable sleep. And easy to say 'Thank you, God,' for all the good things of life. But Leo, what of the difficult portions of life? Can we be in the depths of despair and still be warmed by God's love? If so, then we know perfect joy. When our souls are in torment, can we say 'Thank you, God' and mean it in our hearts? We should welcome our tribulations for they can bring us closer to God, they can strengthen us. There are no problems, Brother Leo, there is only God."

Seeing the Whole Enchilada

On a Wednesday evening, the day before New Year's Eve, Rebecca and I went to a goal setting workshop. It seemed fitting to do at the end of the year.

The workshop leader, Ned Buratovich, was funny and energetic. He shared some good concepts around goal setting, but it wasn't until the end of the evening that I found the best idea.

Ned put up a poster. It was big, almost 3 feet by 4 feet. At the top it said, "One of These Days. . ." Below was a grid of 100 squares, 3 inches by 3 inches. Inside each square, in tiny print, was a full calendar of a year.

The whole poster was a calendar for one hundred years, from 1950 to 2050.

Ned said, "You can see your whole lifetime at a glance with this. When you think, 'I'll get around to doing that project one of these days,' looking at this calendar might help you see how quickly the years go by."

I was stunned by the concept. My entire life and more at a glance. I wanted one of those posters. Ned generously gave one to everyone who attended the workshop.

By noon the next day, the poster was on a wall where I would see it many times a day. I added another row of years so the calendar would start at 1940 instead of 1950 (as I am moving rapidly toward geezerhood).

Some people might find the calendar depressing — they see how much of their life has passed by already, maybe they haven't accomplished as much as they'd

wanted to, it may look as though their best years are
behind them.

I'm sure I'll have moments like that, but another
interpretation provides inspiration—being reminded
that our time here is finite, we have a choice about how
we spend it, starting right now. Today. I ask myself,
"Am I focused on those things that reflect my most
important values?" As I look at the years to come, do I
see them as an ominous void, or as a canvas on which
to paint my future?

The calendar invites reflection. Here are the years I
went to school, here are the nine years I taught college.
(Yikes, look at that, almost a decade; that's quite a
chunk.) Here's where my son Alex was born. Here's
when I moved to California (twenty years ago already;
amazing).

Looking at this one hundred year calendar allows
me to turn inward and to think about my life in general or to remember special times. It's like a telescope
that sees back into the past and forward to the open-
ness and potential of the future.

"The Broken Pot"
A Sufi Story

A water bearer in India delivered water in two large pots that he balanced on a long pole across his shoulders. One pot was sturdy, but the other pot had a crack in it. In the time it took the water bearer to walk from the stream to the master's house, the flawed pot lost half of its water. This went on every day for two years.

The sturdy pot was proud that it did its job so perfectly. The flawed pot was ashamed of itself. Finally, it spoke to the water bearer as he was filling it at the stream.

"I must apologize to you. I am embarrassed," the pot said.

"Why? What's wrong?" asked the water bearer.

"I'm broken. It's no secret. I can't hold all the water you put in me. I lose half of it as you walk to the master's house. I'm of no use to you."

The water bearer nodded. "I understand. But as we deliver the water today, I want you notice the flowers growing by the side of the road."

The pot agreed, and on the path to the master's house, it saw a long row of beautiful flowers. But it was still depressed because once again, at the end of the journey, it had lost half of its water. Again, it apologized.

The water bearer smiled. "Did you notice there were flowers only on your side and not on the other? I've known about the crack in you all along. I decided to take advantage of it by planting flower seeds on your side of the path. You water the flowers every day. I've been picking the flowers and giving them to my master to put around the house. If you didn't have your flaw, he wouldn't be able to enjoy the beauty of fresh flowers. And they give me pleasure too—I see them every day as I walk the path. Because of your crack, I'm able to do and experience something I wouldn't be able to if you didn't have it."

We are all flawed vessels. Like the pot, we're ashamed and embarrassed by our flaws. If we could see past them as failures and ask how we can use them to our advantage, if we could learn to embrace them instead of pushing them away, we too could create beauty in the world for others. Our flaws can be the source of our strength.

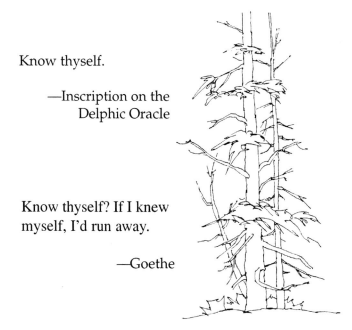

Know thyself.

—Inscription on the
Delphic Oracle

Know thyself? If I knew myself, I'd run away.

—Goethe

Man's main task in life is to give
birth to himself.

—Enrich Fromm

4: GRATITUDE

"The Frogs Choose a King"
FromÆsop's Fables

If the only prayer you say in your whole life is "Thank You," that would suffice.

—Meister Eckhart

How often do we forget to be grateful for what we have and instead covet what others have that we don't? And what's the typical result of that?

Many stories in many cultures reflect this theme. Here's my retelling of one of Aesop's fables.

Once upon a time, there was a pond that was filled with loud and quarrelsome frogs. Nothing ever pleased them; they could always find something wrong to complain about.

Frogs that left the pond and returned brought back stories of two-legged beings that were ruled by kings. Kings were regal and resplendent and beautiful to look at. The frogs decided they needed a king and began praying to God to send them one.

Their croaking prayers were loud, constant and annoying. Their prayers drove all the nearby animals away, to look for another watering-hole.

After ignoring them for a long time, God finally became impatient with their noise.

"So they want a king, do they?" He mused, and flicked a grain of sand out of the heavens. A grain of sand to God is a huge boulder to us, and that boulder fell into the pond with a tremendous explosion.

The croaking stopped. The frog pond was silent. All the frogs were impressed. "Wow," they thought, "now *that's* a king." For a while, all the frogs were quiet and well-behaved. Their king sat silent, unmoving, on the bottom of the pond.

Over time, the frogs approached their king, timidly at first, then more boldly. A few of the adolescent frogs who had no respect for anyone jumped on top of the king. Nothing happened.

Finally, a few frogs began to complain. "He sure doesn't look very regal," said one. "He's so passive." said another. "He doesn't act much like a king."

So the frogs began to pray to God again, lamenting that their king was a fraud and that they wanted, deserved, a real king. Again, the noise was raucous and unending.

God sighed and frowned. "So they don't like their king? Too passive, eh? Right."

And God sent them a crocodile.

The crocodile arrived silently. He certainly was not passive, and he paid a lot of attention to his subjects.

And thereafter the frog pond was quiet.

The moral is, be careful what you wish for, you just might get it.

Dolly Parton Is My Spiritual Leader

"The way I see it, if you want the rainbow, you gotta put up with the rain."
        —Dolly Parton, country singer and actor

I've been reading a motivational book recently, *Get What You Want!* by professional speaker Patricia Fripp. I came across this fascinating little story.

Actress Sally Field was being interviewed about her 1989 film, *Steel Magnolias.* "It was so hot," she said. "We were sweating, wearing these thick wool suits, and we were really complaining. Then I looked over at Dolly and there she was, just smiling. I said, 'Dolly, why aren't you complaining?' She told me, 'When I was young and poor, I wanted to grow up to be rich and famous. I promised myself that if ever I was, I'd never complain about anything.'"

Fripp goes on:

No job, no lifestyle, no situation comes without inconveniences and disadvantages. If you get what you asked for and grumble, you're not going to get any sympathy from me. You'll never achieve something that makes you happy if you don't start by being happy with what you've achieved.

What's incredible about the Dolly Parton story isn't the promise she made—we've all made similar prom-

ises many times ("Please God, just give me . . . ," or
"Let me . . . , and I'll never . . . again," or "I'll always . .
. from now on."). What's incredible is that she didn't
forget her promise. Obviously, she's made a real effort
to keep it, and she's successful at keeping it.

Most of our personal promises are silent, secret
pacts, and we don't tell anyone. So they're easier to
break. No one knows the promise but ourselves. Never
mind that broken promises, even secret ones, erode our
self-esteem.

It's the heart of Dolly's promise that's also mean-
ingful. It's about gratitude.

It's about seeing what's working, rather than
what's not working. Think of the people in the world
who would gladly cut off their arm to live in our
house, to eat what we eat, to drive the car we drive, to
have the job we have, and on and on. If we *really*
thought about it, we'd be prostrate with gratitude for
the life we have. Instead, we take our lives for granted
and complain about what's missing.

Dolly's got it exactly right. From our viewpoint, it
looks like she's got it made: stardom, riches, adulation.
But you can bet that from her point of view, lots of
other actors are younger and slimmer, get better parts,
get more money than she. She could envy Cher, or Julia
Roberts, or Michelle Pfeiffer. Instead, she focuses on
what's working with the life she has. No complaints.

I'm going to buy a huge poster of Dolly Parton and
put it up in my office. And when Rebecca asks me
what this is about, I'll say that Dolly is my new spiritual leader. I wonder if I can get away with it. I can
hear Rebecca now: "You want a spiritual leader? Here's
a poster of Mother Teresa."

Not quite the same.

"The Woman Who Walked To Paradise"
A Modern Version of an Old Folktale

Once upon a time there was a woman who lived in Silicon Valley. She worked as a marketing manager for a successful start-up company. She was divorced and had a son, eight, who lived with her and visited his dad on weekends. She drove a BMW and owned a condo close to the hills of the state game refuge west of Interstate 280.

She was not a happy woman. Loneliness, work pressures, commute traffic, hassles with her ex-husband, communication problems with her son, aging issues, weight-loss struggles, aging parents, credit card debt, money-management issues—life was overwhelming.

One day, in desperation, she called a phone psychic who claimed to be a reincarnation of Teddy Roosevelt.

"I'll tell you the truth," the psychic said.

"Go ahead," the woman said, thinking of the $3.99 a minute she was paying for the call.

"Paradise is nearby. It's in the west. Look for it. It exists and you will go to it."

"Oh bull," the woman said and hung up. "What trash," she thought. But as the weeks went by, she found herself thinking about paradise more and more. She wanted to believe in it, she hungered for it to be real.

As she walked down the main street of her town day after day, looking into the same stores, Chili's, The Gap, Barnes & Noble, and Starbucks, everything looked trite and phony and old and boring. She felt like throwing a brick through a plate-glass window.

At night, standing on her patio, she thought she could see a faint glow in the sky beyond the hills to the west.

"That's it," she told herself, "that's paradise. I'm so sick of this life, I want out."

One afternoon soon after that, she snapped. She came out of a store, rushing to get back to work, to find a parking ticket on the windshield of her Beemer. She'd forgotten to feed the meter.

"That's it," she yelled, throwing her new shoes at her car, "I'm outta here." As she walked away, she called her sister on her cell phone. "Pick up my son," she screamed and heaved the phone at a passing truck. She was going to paradise.

By sunset she had reached the crest of the western hills. She was dirty, sweaty and scratched. Her slacks and shoes were ruined, her legs ached, but damn it, she was going to paradise and she was close now. All she had to do was hike down the far side of the hill. It was getting too dark to see her way through the under-brush and woods. She decided to sleep and walk into paradise in the morning.

She built herself a little bed of pine boughs and took off her ruined shoes, pointing them to the west, toward paradise.

As she drifted off to sleep, she imagined the beauty, the joy, the serenity she would know in the morning.

In the darkest, deepest part of the night, an imp, a gnome (well-known in Silicon Valley for creating computer glitches), crept out of the bushes and examined the sleeping figure. Then, because it was his nature to be perverse, he turned her shoes to face in the opposite direction.

The woman woke up as the sky began to lighten. She was too excited to wait until dawn. She pulled on her torn shoes and stumbled off through the bushes and trees, heading downhill.

Finally, she saw lights in the valley ahead. "There it is," she laughed, "there's paradise." She came out of the woods and as dawn broke, she walked into paradise.

That's funny, she thought, it looks a lot like the dumb town I just left. What kind of paradise is this?

She became more confused as she wandered the empty streets. Everything looked the same—Chili's, The Gap, Barnes & Noble, and Starbucks. "Starbucks in paradise? It can't be!" she muttered. Everything looked as trite and phony and boring as her old town. What was going on?

Was paradise a parallel universe? Was it a hologram of an image from her memory? If so, why not Paris or New Orleans? How strange.

Finally, she stood in front of a familiar-looking condo and felt sure that inside there was an eight-year-old who looked and talked just like her son.

What was she to do? She looked closely at everything around her. What if this really were paradise? What if this was it? She looked hard, as if she were trying to see into the bricks and trees and parked cars and grass growing in the cracks of the sidewalk.

"Well," she finally thought, squaring her shoulders, "if this is paradise, then it's not all it's cracked up to be. Still, I'd better make the most of it. I didn't come all this way for nothing."

And from that day on, she was a much happier woman.

Gratitude is heaven itself.
—William Blake

5: LOVE

Left and Gone Away

Let yourself be silently drawn by the pull of what you really love.

—Rumi

I'm still troubled by the recent deaths of Joe DiMaggio, Stanley Kubrick, and Gene Siskel. I understand my reaction to Kubrick's passing, because he directed my favorite movie, *2001: A Space Odyssey*. And Siskel seemed like a friend, someone I knew and felt comfortable with. But DiMaggio? I never saw him play; Mickey Mantle had taken his place in center field when I first got interested in baseball. I guess it's the image of the man—playing ball with such grace and apparent ease that it took people's breath away. They say his ball playing was nothing short of magnificent.

As was Stanley Kubrick's movie making. He moved with equal grace, creating images of light, sound and movement that also took people's breath away, as happened to me the first time I saw *2001*. Magnificent.

Richard Schickel captured the source of Kubrick's magnificence in an article in *Time* magazine: "Kubrick . . . was haunted by life's brevity, by the hopelessness of transcending the blighted human condition within the short span allotted us. . . . There was art, that fragile fortress men like him erect against mortality. If one could just build it carefully enough." That is, if we can be magnificent enough, we might hold off the grim reaper.

DiMaggio and Kubrick were distant heroes, far away on Olympus. I wouldn't have known what to say had I met either of them. Gene Siskel, though, seemed like a regular guy, someone I could have a beer with. He was like a neighbor, someone who came over and hung out in my kitchen every Sunday evening and told me about the latest movies he'd seen. Magnificent might be too strong a word for that, but not too strong to describe his passion for film. He was on fire when he talked about movies he loved.

My wife and I and two other couples meet regularly to discuss spiritual books we're reading or other topics that interest us. Barry, one of our group, said he'd heard someone on the radio talk about magnificence: everyone ought to think about what it is they're magnificent at. Barry said, "We could all do that as an exercise. Next time we meet, we could each share what it is we think we're magnificent at." The room was silent. A few heads nodded, but the next time we met, we "didn't have time" to bring up the topic. I was glad.

I'd given it a moment's thought, but that was all. I don't seem to measure up to the dictionary definition of the word: "Strikingly beautiful or impressive"—that was DiMaggio; "impressive to the mind or spirit; sublime"—that was Kubrick; "imposing, larger-than-life, awe-inspiring"—both DiMaggio and Kubrick.

Compared to DiMaggio and Kubrick, my job, and probably your job, can seem like small potatoes. Nobody gives us a standing ovation; we don't take people's breath away (unless we goof up big time), and nobody cares what we think about the latest flick. How can we "build a fortress against mortality?"

We can build it through our relationships. Our fortress is our capacity to love. We can genuinely love our family and closest friends. We can love them in a way that they know they're loved. To be love in action, not just thought, that's magnificence.

Our magnificence doesn't shine on the baseball diamond or in the movie theater; it shines whenever we're with our loved ones.

Joltin' Joe has left the ballpark.

Stanley has left the set.

For Gene, the balcony is closed.

For us, the game isn't over yet.

Lessons From the Butterfly Man

In my work as a business presentations coach, I have observed an interesting phenomenon. When a speaker, let's call him George, is nervous and unsure of himself, he tends to contract, as though he wants to make himself smaller. (To become a smaller target?) Even his voice becomes smaller.

But when George is comfortable and confident, he uses larger gestures, his voice becomes louder, and he employs more movement.

We can talk about these two states in terms of contraction and expansion. We can also attribute other qualities to these states. When we're in a state of contraction, we're trying to control a situation so that it goes well. We're holding on tight (to the lectern, perhaps). In expansion, we've let go of control and are willing to respond to whatever happens. In contraction, we resist. In expansion, we release.

There's a heaviness to contraction, a movement downward as well as inward. There's a lightness to expansion, a movement upward as well as outward.

In contraction, there's a struggle to look good and not appear foolish. We may be striving for perfection. In expansion, there's a willingness to be oneself, to be genuine. There's a willingness to be imperfect and make mistakes.

When we're in contraction, everything is pretty serious, even grim. When we're in expansion, we see the humor in situations, including our own.

When we're in contraction, we lose an awareness of what's happening around us. In expansion, we regain that awareness. Our field of vision is larger.

How do these two states relate to our lives outside of public speaking? Very well, I contend.

Any time we're upset, angry, afraid, or experiencing negative emotions, we're in a state of contraction. Feeling stressed pushes us toward contraction.

Any time we have an argument, we're in contraction. When we hold a grudge, stay resentful, and aren't honest about our feelings, we're in contraction. The definition of contraction describing George, the public speaker, holds true for us in our work and social situations.

Think of the common term, lighten up, not metaphorically, but literally. If a friend says it to us, it's usually because we're in a state of contraction (anger, fear, defensiveness, etc.). We're being urged to shift to a state of expansion, which is a lighter state than contraction.

We may shift from contraction to expansion and back again quickly and often, many times in a single day.

You may have grown up feeling that you didn't have a choice about being in contraction or expansion. I know I grew up with that belief. If bad things happened or a friend said something I interpreted as critical, I went into contraction. "I can't help it, that's how I am," I would whine. I felt controlled *by* my emotions, not in control of them.

Now I know that emotions are always a choice. Always. Our choice. We're always choosing to either expand or contract. It may not often feel like a choice, but it is.

In his book, *The Lazy Man's Guide to Enlightenment,* Thaddeus Golas describes the states of expansion and contraction and contends that the primary, in fact the *only* route to shifting from contraction to expansion is by becoming more open to love.

Sound too airy-fairy?

Here's a personal experience to illustrate my point. In 1980, I decided to become a street performer at Fisherman's Wharf in San Francisco. As romantic as the art form was, I was never really comfortable with this kind of performing. I found it hard to get people to stop, then hard to get them to stay to the end of my act (I told stories for kids). During one week at Pier 39, I had a bout of stage fright that contracted me so much I had stomach aches. I didn't want to show up, and I didn't want to do my act. I wanted to quit.

So I went to the Butterfly Man who looked after all the performers on the pier. He was a street performer himself, a juggler. I've never known anyone able to work a street crowd better than he. The more people heckled him, the more he insulted them back and the more they loved it. Hundreds of people would surround him when he performed. He was fantastic. He made a lot of money with his shows, too.

I explained to him how afraid I was to perform. He was silent for a few seconds, then he said, "You need to love your audience."

I didn't know what he meant.

"Just love them," he said again, and looked at me hard. I didn't get it. How could I love something that frightened the heck out of me?

I know now that he was saying the same thing as Thaddeus Golas in *The Lazy Man's Guide to Enlightenment*: When we're in contraction, we need to turn our mental state around. Don't fear the audience, let that go. When we truly love someone, we are in big-time expansion. We want to expand so much that we merge with the beloved.

When someone ticks us off, instead of complaining about what a jerk he is (contraction), we can choose to be grateful for the gift—the opportunity to turn contraction into expansion by accepting what is happening. Our lives can be our spiritual classroom. We have opportunities to practice every day.

We do not
try to
discover
something
new, but to
recover
that which
is lost.

—G.I. Gurdjieff

6: OUR INNER CRITIC

Lessons From a Cat

There is no snooze button on a cat who wants breakfast.

—Anonymous

Thousands of years ago, cats were worshipped as gods. Cats have never forgotten this.

—Anonymous

We lost our cat last week. Don't worry, this isn't going to be a maudlin "I love cats don't you love cats?" piece. It's about managing stress.

California, our cat, was 16 years old. We moved five times in those 16 years, and California adjusted easily to each new home. He was a mellow, laid-back fellow, which may explain his longevity. He didn't suffer from stress. Even when he got locked in a closet accidentally, he waited patiently until we came to look for him.

Now that he's gone, I'm struck with the power of pets to relieve human stress. You've probably read articles about people with high blood pressure given dogs or cats to pet and hold. After five minutes, their blood pressure dropped. As I walk around the house and remember "That was where California liked to sun himself," I realize how much his mere presence put me at ease. Pets don't have to be curled in our laps to lower our stress.

Dr. Meyer Friedman, the cardiologist who coined the term "Type A Behavior," is a strong advocate for pets as stress reducers.

Sure, they take time, they get sick and they don't always behave as we think they ought, but that's true of all relationships. Pets don't care how much money we have or what we look like (although they do care that their food arrives on time). And they rarely complain. Even when they're sick, they go off by themselves.

I was also struck with the power of my negative mind-chatter after California died. As he aged, I was clear that I wanted to hold him in my arms when the end came. On a Tuesday, I could see he was sick, and I made an appointment with our vet for 4:30. I had a coaching appointment with a client at 2:00. There was plenty of time to get back, I thought. But the client wanted additional coaching, so I called Rebecca and asked her to take California to the vet in my place.

California died while the vet was holding and examining him.

That night, and the next day, and at odd moments since, my self-talk went something like: "Good going, Sport. You wanted to be with California when he died. You had the chance, and you blew it." Bam! Pow! Sock! My inner critic hit me with some low blows.

"Why weren't you quicker to pick up on the clues about how sick he was?" Bam! again.

"Why didn't you take him to the vet a day earlier?" Another pounding blow.

"You could have continued the coaching the next day. You could have come home. You could have been there." A left jab. A right cross to the head. Bam, bam!

I tried to respond with the Zen monk's question, "Is that so?" At other times, I'd think, "Ah, my old friends, the voices of guilt and shame are at it again, pounding me." I even told them to shut up.

I was able to avoid spiraling into depression, but I had some bad moments. What worked for me at those times was to get up, go into the back yard, and get into some intense digging in the garden until my back ached. It's a trick of shifting the mind by shifting the body.

Rebecca also helped me reframe my thoughts. She suggested that by her taking California to the vet instead of me, it helped her to realize how much he meant to her. Maybe it was the right thing. It was my scenario to be present at California's final moments, not his.

No matter how good we get at managing our negative, judgmental self-talk, it can still turn ugly when we screw up. But we can learn to let it go —cats and dogs do.

Cats seem to go on the principle that it never does any harm to ask for what you want.

—Joseph Wood Krutch

"You There! The Voice In My Head! Shut Up!"

L ately I've been more aware of my mind's nega-tive thoughts than I used to be: "Oh, there I go again, making up negative interpretations of events and making assumptions."

A good example concerned a workshop I wanted to attend. One of the days was scheduled to go from 10 AM to 7 PM. My wife Rebecca and I had a long-stand-ing dinner date with another couple to celebrate our anniversaries on that night. I called the workshop leader and left a message to explain my situation and to say that I wanted to leave the workshop by 5:00. I got back a message that that was unsatisfactory, and I would need to talk to him directly.

From that moment on, my negative mind took over and ran various scripts of the upcoming phone conver-sation. The scripts revolved around being told I *had* to stay for the full time (being told what I could and couldn't do), and around my telling him what he could do with his workshop. Righteous indignation can really feel good. I noticed a tension in my chest and a tightness in my shoulder muscles as I played and replayed this imaginary conversation. My body was reacting as though I was really talking to the leader. I knew what was happening, but I found it extremely difficult to turn the tape loop off; it kept repeating and repeating and repeating.

At the same time, I happened to pick up a book called *The Heart's Code: Tapping the Wisdom and Power of Our Heart Energy* by Paul Pearsall, a clinical and educational psychologist. Pearsall wrote:

> In its potentially lethal convenant with its
> body, the brain never shuts up. It is designed to be
> constantly on some level of alert. . . . It is in a state
> of perpetual readiness to react, defend, or attack
> when it or its body senses threats—real or not.
> The brain-body covenant is one designed prima-
> rily for staying alive, seeking stimulation, doing,
> and getting. . . .
>
> The brain is self-protective and territorial. Its
> code is 'I, me, mine.' A natural pessimist, it
> evolved to expect and anticipate the worst as a
> form of self-defense left over from our primitive
> ancestors' necessary constant vigilance for outside
> threats.

Pearsall sure had my brain pegged right. I saw how
my mind had leaped to protect me from an imagined
assault on my inalienable right to leave a workshop
early. Interestingly, even though I understood the
worthlessness of what I was doing, my mind still
wanted to play out the confrontational scene over and
over. Obviously, I had a charge on this imagined insult.

I knew my only salvation would be to have the real
conversation as quickly as possible. Finally, the moment of truth came. My body was tense (of course). I
was ready for an argument, and I wasn't going to back
down. The workshop leader said, "I'd really like you to
stay, but if you feel you need to go, that's fine. What
can I do to help you catch up on the material you'll
miss?"

Did I hear that right? I wanted to yell, "Oh no you
don't, Buster. I've spent a lot of time and energy creating this conversation, and you're not going to rob me
of it. It would mean all that time and energy was
wasted."

Actually, I was relieved. But it's true, the time and energy spent was wasted. Wasted big time.

Pearsall again: "In effect, the brain drags your body with it to do its bidding, hauling you and your heart along on its rough ride, whether or not you are sure 'in your heart' that you want to go where it is taking you."

There are some good lessons for me in this one:

1. I'm glad I was able to identify the negative voice as that and not blindly accept it as speaking the "truth."

2. I'm glad I was able to keep from getting down on myself for not being able to shut off the voice.

3. I'm glad I was aware of my physical reactions to the mind's upset. My body cued me that something was terribly wrong with where my mind was going.

4. Next time my negative mind begins playing tapes—and there *will* be a next time—I'll be better equipped to laugh at it and not take it so seriously.

Ironically, one member of our party got sick and the dinner was cancelled. So I stayed until the end of the session. Oh boy.

Lessons From Stanley

In the night I am constantly haunted by what I am trying to realize. I rise broken with fatigue each morning. But the coming of dawn gives me courage.

—Claude Monet

Have you seen the movie "Wag the Dog"? If not, here's the basic plot: the President is accused of sexual misconduct (this is too obvious to even comment on), and it's only two weeks until the election. His handlers are afraid that the scandal might cost him the presidency.

Enter a spin doctor (Robert DeNiro) who has a plan that a threat of war would take the media's attention off the scandal. He asks Stanley, a Hollywood producer (Dustin Hoffman), to help create the phony war.

Stanley has boundless enthusiasm and confidence. Every time it looks like their flimsy but elaborate plan is about to fall apart, Stanley yells, "THIS IS NOTHING!"

Stanley is unstoppable. With every crisis, he comes up with a way out. His confidence is unshakeable. He is the model of chutzpah.

He was my hero in the film. I thought, I want this guy around when I run into tough times. When my own confidence turns to mush at 2 AM, or when I'm staring down the gun barrel of a sudden disappointment or challenge, I want Stanley at my side yelling, "THIS IS NOTHING!"

Just last week, I gave a talk on stress management to an association. I went to their convention a day early to meet people. It didn't take long to realize that while these were warm and wonderful individuals, I had little in common with them.

I knew what I had to say about stress was relevant to them, but I didn't have a clue how to connect with them at the start. Without that I wouldn't be very successful.

What can I say, I wondered. They are yin and I am yang. The evening dinner speaker confirmed my fears by speaking eloquently from the core of their yin values and beliefs. The audience gave him a standing ovation.

Oh man. My yang heart sank. I was going to bomb. Big time. (My mind jumped to the worst case possible —it wouldn't just be bad, it would be a catastrophe.)

I went back to my room and called Rebecca, who calmed me down and reminded me of a story I've told countless times that was within their belief system. Wow. Problem solved just like that.

The next morning I opened with that story, they smiled and nodded, and the talk was successful.

Rebecca had saved me. She had played the role of Stanley (though she never yelled, "THIS IS NOTH-ING!").

We all need a Stanley at various moments in our lives. And we need to speak up, as I did, to ask for advice, for help. Stanleys are great coaches, but they aren't mind readers.

If Rebecca hadn't been available, I hope I would have had the presence of mind to sit, breathe deeply, calm down, and be my own Stanley and think of the story that I needed. I knew the story well; fear had buried it.

In the movie, Stanley was undone at the end by his ego, which turned out to be as big as his confidence. Sometimes people in my stress workshops worry that developing too much confidence could be negative, that it would result in their becoming self-centered. I tell them that self-centeredness isn't real confidence, it's fear masquerading as confidence. Confident people who have ego-strength don't need to shout, "Look at me." They're generally quiet and modest.

And they don't make good characters in movies. Not interesting enough. I think there's not much danger that those of us who want to be more confident need to fear becoming a Stanley. That fear is a trick our mind plays on us to keep us from developing our confidence.

Worrying? Anxious? Fearful? Doubting? "THIS IS NOTHING!"

Another Lesson From Stanley

After writing about Stanley in the previous chapter, I wondered whether I would have any need for his sage advice ("THIS IS NOTHING!") in the near future.

Well, wouldn't you know . . . a few days later, Arianne, my college student office assistant, left me a note saying that she had taken a full-time job for the summer and could only work evenings for me. I had assumed that since she wasn't going to summer school, she would be working *extra* hours. I'd fantasized about the many career-orbiting projects she could help me with. Then this. Argh.

Immediately, the negative chatter popped up: "Evenings aren't as good as days. She'll be too tired from her day job to work. She'll want to go out nights with her boyfriend. I'll never see her. There go the projects. My career will stagnate."

My negative mind chatter about the recent death of my cat, California, had a heaviness to it, a sadness. I fought it by busying myself with hard physical labor and getting out of the house. This self-talk was different. It sounded shrill, nagging, almost petty. I needed a different strategy.

Enter Stanley.

My imaginary conversation with Stanley went something like this:

Me: "This is terrible. I'm losing my assistant."

Stanley: "This is nothing. If she had quit with no notice and you found out that she hadn't paid your bills in months, and your account was overdrawn and hopelessly fouled up, then you could worry."

Me: "No, really this is serious. I have important stuff . . ."

Stanley: "This is nothing. If she had quit and you found that she had renamed all your computer files in some Byzantine code, or if she had purged all your files leaving you with blank cyberspace, then you could worry."

Me: "Okay, it's not like that. But I won't be able to . . ."

Stanley: "This is nothing. If she had quit and sued you for sexual harassment and slapped you with a paternity suit, and called the IRS, claiming you've been cheating big-time on your taxes, then you could worry."

Finally, I gave up and laughed. Stanley had done his job well. He managed to shut down my mind's prattle.

Naturally, when I did talk to Arianne, all my fears were unfounded. Of course. That's how it is with negative mind chatter.

Thanks, Stanley. Come back and visit anytime.

Life shrinks or expands
according to one's courage.

—Anais Nin

7: PEACE AND SERENITY

Peace, Be Still

I recently returned from a silent retreat at my Unity church's headquarters in Missouri. It was a powerful experience. I want to share one part of it that's related to stress.

I arrived at 6 PM on a Saturday evening. I was tired from the previous week's work, but determined to wring every possible drop of value from this retreat. I got up at 5 A.M. on Sunday, took my 30 minute walk, did some yoga and reading, and was ready for the events of the day. To my amazement, I kept nodding off in both the morning and afternoon sessions. By dinnertime I was really annoyed with myself. How was I going to get anything from this retreat if I slept through it? The fact that the retreat leaders told us from the beginning to go easy, to take care of ourselves, to not try to go to all the sessions if we didn't want to, made no difference. I was going to do it all and get it all. On Monday, I got it all right.

That morning, a retreat leader told the story of Jesus and his disciples who were in a boat on a lake when a storm came up. Jesus was asleep, but his disciples were going nuts with fear that the boat would sink and they would drown. They yelled at Jesus about how could he be sleeping at a terrible time like this. Jesus woke up and said "Peace, be still," and the storm stopped.

I had heard that story time and again over the years and it never made much sense to me. The retreat leader asked us to look at it from a metaphysical perspective: the disciples can represent various aspects of ourselves. The storm is all the dreadful, horrendous things that can happen to us (finances, job, relationships, etc.). When the storm hits, we get upset, fearful, angry, defensive, and all of our voices, our interior committee, start screaming and arguing. If we listen to the words "Peace, be still," and calm down, the storm that appears so dangerous in our minds will subside, and we can deal with what's real.

I got that I had been playing the disciples since I arrived and had created my own storm of time urgency. I got that I was tense and stressed out and that I was running from event to event, not being very conscious or mindful of my surroundings or the people around me. The whole point of the retreat was to stop doing and start being. The point was to stand still and go inside, into the great and peaceful quiet.

From that moment on, the quieter I became, the more meaning the retreat had for me.

Now I am back home, wondering how I might keep some of the peacefulness I experienced. One way will be to remember the words, "Peace, be still," not only when I start getting whipped up over the things that aren't working, but to think it often, throughout the day.

This morning my minister quoted a Buddhist prayer that I'll also try to remember: "May I be at peace; may my heart remain open."

Afterword: After I drafted this article, I went shopping for a new watch. The one with the functions I wanted also had the word "Stop" on it in big letters. My first inclination was to reject it. Why would I want a watch that said "Stop." Then I realized that it was the perfect watch for someone who wanted to remember to stop and be still. Now I've got a perfect little reminder.

The Big Little Pause

God's one and only voice is silence.

—Herman Melville

W e often lament that we don't have enough downtime in our lives. It's all rush, rush, rush.

We could find a lot more downtime if we'd be willing to accept it in small portions. Granted, it's almost impossible to find an hour to spare. Even half an hour can be rough. But how about ten seconds? Five seconds?

Your first thought might be, what the heck could I do with that? In five seconds you could take one deep breath. A deep breath helps us relax. It turns us inward. It quiets us. It momentarily stops the mind's constant chatter.

Typically we think of pauses as meaningless, like dead air on the radio. Artists don't think of pauses that way. They see the value of what isn't happening in the context of what is happening.

In dance, the dancer's arm swings up and stops momentarily, then swings down. What has occurred in that moment of nothing, that moment of balance, of equilibrium?

A snapshot is created. A shape, a sculpture is revealed. There's contrast, dramatic effect, even surprise.

Consider the pauses in a speech. A speaker can

draw us into the speech more deeply with silence, the absence of sound. We have time to think, to feel.

Writers create pauses, too. They use space to do it. The space at the end of a chapter is a long pause. The space at the end of a paragraph is a shorter one. Consider the meaning in this pause: "She leaned forward and gave him —a kiss." Poetry gains meaning by the value of the silence in contrast to the spoken word. (Poetry needs to be read aloud to bring it to life, to experience the shifting relationship of sound and silence.)

Music. A jazz musician called pauses "God moments." The famed pianist Arthur Rubenstein was once asked by a woman, "How do you handle the notes as well as you do?"

He replied, "Madam, I handle the notes no better than others, but the pauses—ah, that is where the art resides."

In comic art, the little space between panels (comic artists call it the gutter) is where our minds make connections and inferences from panel to panel.

Think of the tiny pause between the punch line of a joke and the laughter of the listener. A lot happens in that brief moment.

When I asked my yoga teacher about pauses, the first thing he said was, "And a hush falls over the crowd." Yes, that's it.

These moments of pause, balance, and equilibrium are always there. Notice them. Create them. Enjoy them. Let them relax you.

"Finding Perfect Peace"
A Folktale

Once upon a time, a king in a far-off land became preoccupied with the concept of peace. He wanted a painting of perfect peace to hang in his throne room to inspire him. He invited artists throughout the kingdom to submit their renditions.

He received many paintings, studied them all, and rejected all but two. One was a beautiful painting of a quiet lake in front of a majestic mountain on a sunny day. As the king looked at it, he felt a rush of calmness well up within him. It made him smile. It was beautiful. Everyone in the court agreed that this was indeed a picture of perfect peace.

The second painting was not so beautiful. It also had a majestic mountain, but the day was not sunny. The skies were dark and foreboding. A waterfall spilled down the jagged rocky slopes of the mountain. Looking at this painting was troubling to the king. He wondered why he was even considering it. It wasn't about peace at all. Yet, it intrigued him for some reason. Everyone in the court made rude comments under their breaths. They thought the artist was crazy.

The king looked closely at the painting. Then he noticed something. Behind the waterfall, the artist had painted a tiny bird sitting in a tiny nest in a scrawny bush growing out of a cleft in the granite. The angry waters rushed by, but the bird sat, unruffled . . . in peace. The king felt an even greater sense of warmth and centeredness in his body.

He turned to his aides and noblemen who were

watching him closely. "I choose the second painting as the most realistic portrayal of peace," he said. There was a murmur throughout the court. The king explained:

"It's easy to be at peace when life is good and the road is smooth. But when we are able to be at peace in the midst of turmoil, when we can remain calm when there is noise and strife and conflict, ah, my friends, that is the real meaning of peace."

If you have
a garden
and a
library,
you have
everything
you need.

—Cicero

8: POINT OF VIEW

The Eyes of Babes

The childhood shows the man,
As morning shows the day.
      —John Milton

A few weeks ago, I was in my favorite neighborhood coffee shop, enjoying a hot cup and the bright early morning. It was my place, a cafe I'd been coming to for over three years. A father came in with his child, about 12-16 months old, in a stroller. They settled into a table next to me.

The child was beautiful, wide-eyed and totally present. While his father read the newspaper and sipped his latte, the boy looked around calmly but intensely and took in everything. I could almost hear the neurons clicking, growing, interconnecting, sending elaborate electrochemical signals across the neuron fibers. He was reading patterns, colors, sounds, making grand interpretations of a vast and wonderful world. If he could talk, I felt he'd be saying "Oh wow!" over and over again. It was beautiful to watch.

Then he turned his head and looked up and over his shoulder. His eyes locked onto something and he held his position, like a bird dog on point. It couldn't have been comfortable for him. I wondered what it was that fascinated him so, and my eyes followed his gaze.

Between the plate glass window and the ceiling was a section of stained glass, about a foot and half high by eight feet long. The morning sun was streaming through it. I stared at it in amazement. *I had never seen it before.* In the more than three years I'd been coming to this coffee house, I had never seen this stained glass. Incredible.

I was reminded of when my son was a child and how he constantly surprised me with what he saw in the world. I miss that. I've lost that way of seeing. Sometimes I get it back for a few moments at a time, but it would be more fun to have a child around to be my guide.

Jill the Witch

W e never know where we'll discover a small insight to help us relieve stress, to help us on our journey.
When I attended a conference a while ago, I stayed with my son Alex at his apartment in Portland.

One of his friends, Greg Dale, has a band called "Jill the Witch." Greg had drawn a kind of poster about the band, and Alex had it hanging on his living room wall.

I slept in the living room on the couch. One morning after the alarm went off and I lay there, still drowsy, the poster caught my eye.

I'd seen the poster many times, but this time was different. (I've read that the moments between sleep and waking are great doorways to the subconscious. This was one of those moments.)

At the top of the poster was the band's name—Jill the Witch. Underneath was a scarecrow stick figure drawing of a witch.

Interestingly, I had just seen an exhibition at the San Jose Museum of Art by Barbara Broughel of, as the brochure stated, "brooms and other household objects of early American design. Each one is a 'portrait' of a person accused, convicted, and/or executed as a witch." The charges against the women ranged from "planning to make merry on Christmas" and "being discontented with her chores" (we're all doomed), to "displaying turbulent passions" and "having power over the imaginations of men."

Greg's drawing had a similar quality to some of the

wrought iron "portraits." (Were the two thinking along similar lines?) Around Greg's "portrait" of Jill were these words:

Learn to love
Learn to live
Learn to die

In that moment I saw the words in a new way—as a perfect expression of a life philosophy. I realized it was my own philosophy—distilled to its essence far better than I'd been able to do.

Learn to love. I want to expand my capacity to love, to stop so many judgments and criticisms that keep me separate from others.

Learn to live. I want to wake up to living more fully in the moment. I do not want to spend my time in guilt, grudges and recriminations of the past, or in worry and fear of the future.

Learn to die. I want to make the big trip with some equanimity and grace. I do not want to go screaming with regret and terror "into that good night." (Stephen Levine's *A Year to Live* is a good guidebook.)

Then I flipped the wording of the ideas from an injunction, from the point of view of the teacher, "Learn to . . . ," to the point of view of those of us who have a deep yearning for something that we can hardly express:

Teach me to love
Teach me to live
Teach me to die

These words could be a morning and evening prayer; thoughts for a meditation. Here is a credo, boiled down to twelve words.

I haven't seen Jill the Witch perform yet, but I want to. Greg, the songwriter and lead singer, is something of a poet/philosopher. I'll wait until I hear his lyrics before I'm ready to compare him to Bob Dylan, but he has a good start.

Funny, isn't it, how we sometimes find important things in odd places. It's sort of like putting on an old pair of sneakers and finding a precious ring.

Keep your radar scope on. Maybe you'll find an important something today. If not today, there's tomorrow or the next day. It's out there, waiting for you.

"The Nature of Illusion"
A Folktale

I love stories. A good story pierces us and changes us. A good story reminds us of some aspect of our humanity. Here's a story about the impermanence of things, the illusion that things last. Our minds create these illusions. To quote from a little book called *The Teaching of Buddha*:

> . . . Every existence or phenomenon arises from the functions of the mind, just as different things appear from the sleeve of a magician. . . . Just as a picture is drawn by an artist, surroundings are created by the activities of the mind. . . . The activities of the mind have no limit; they form the surroundings of life.

The Nature of Illusion

Once there was a yogi, a holy man, who lived a selfless and devout life. When he was old, the Buddha appeared before him.

"Because of how you've lived your life, I want to grant you a wish," the Buddha said.

The yogi thought about it and said, "I want to understand the nature of illusion."

The Buddha shook his head. "Surely you know that already. What do you really want?"

"That is what I truly want."

"Very well, " the Buddha said. "I will need a glass of water from the river. Bring me one."

The yogi found a glass and walked to the river. As he approached it, he passed a farmhouse. The farmer and his family were in the front yard and seemed in distress. The yogi asked what was wrong.

The farmer told him that his rice crop was failing and he didn't know how to save it. If the crop failed, all would be lost.

The yogi said, "I know something about growing rice. Let me see the crop." When he saw the rice, the yogi knew what was wrong. He stayed with the farmer and his family while he tended the rice crop back to health.

Meanwhile, he fell in love with the farmer's oldest daughter. They decided to marry. The farmer was overjoyed and bought the yogi a home with the profits from his now abundant rice crop. Oddly, the yogi seemed to be getting younger as time went by.

The yogi and his wife had a baby, a son. There was great happiness and life was good.

A few years later, a terrible monsoon struck and the river overflowed its banks. The rice farm was inundated, and the yogi stood in the raging waters, holding onto his son and wife. The boy's hand slipped from his grasp. As he lunged to rescue the boy, his wife was carried away by the current. Both wife and son disappeared under the swirling waters. He screamed.

In the next moment the yogi found himself standing on dry land, with a glass of muddy river water in his hand, facing the Buddha.

"Coming Soon to Your Town"
A Folktale

It was a hot, sunny day in the summer of 1946 on a small farm outside of town. An old farmer quietly talked to his mule to encourage her in their plowing. Hour after hour the mule, farmer and plow turned the rich Wisconsin earth.

A car came up the road from the south. It was covered with dust. It stopped when it was opposite the farmer. A man in a white shirt got out and waved the farmer over. The farmed halted his mule and walked slowly over the fresh furrows to the fence. The man nodded and smiled.

"Hi there," he said. "I'm headed up to your town here. Never been there before. I'm looking for a place to settle down. Tell me, what kind of folks live in this town?"

The farmer rested one hand on a fence post. "Well," he asked, "what kind of folks were there in the place where you came from?"

The man laughed without smiling. "What kind? The cheatin' lyin' kind, that's what. You couldn't trust 'em at all. A bunch of thievin' snakes is what they were. That's why I left, couldn't stand to be around 'em any longer."

The farmer paused, squinting off across his field. "Well," he said slowly, "I reckon those are the kind of folks you'll find in this town."

The man in the white shirt snorted, frowning. "I knew it," he said loudly. "Much obliged, stranger. I'll keep on looking. I'll find me a place."

As he got in his car, he yelled back to the farmer: "This country's going to hell in a handbasket."

The old farmer went back to his plowing.

A few hours later, another dusty car came up the road and stopped. A man in a blue shirt got out and called to the farmer.

He stopped his mule again and walked over to the fence, wiping his face with a bandanna. It sure was a hot day.

"Afternoon," the man said tilting his head. "Sorry to disturb you. I'd like to ask you a question."

"Shoot," the farmer said, and wiped his face again, then wiped the sweat band inside his hat.

"I need to find a place to live. I was thinkin' of moving into this town here. I'm wondering what the people are like."

The farmer put his hat back on and stuffed the bandanna in his back pocket. "What were the people like where you came from?"

The man sighed. "Oh, they were nice people. Real nice. Friendly, eager to help. I had a lot of good friends. I hated to leave, actually. Wish I could of stayed."

The farmer nudged a clod of dirt with the toe of his work shoe. "Well, I reckon that's the kind of folks you'll find in this town."

The man in the blue shirt smiled. "Thank you, sir. I'll go on up and have a look."

As the man drove away, the old farmer slowly walked back to his plow and mule.

It sure was a hot one, no doubt about it.

It's kind of fun to do the impossible.

—Walt Disney

9: MINDFULNESS

I'm In My Seat,
But My Mind Has Left the Building

Everything in the universe is within you. Ask all from
yourself.

—Rumi

A coaching client of mine has asked me for some
tips on becoming more mindful.
The place to start is by answering "What the
heck does 'mindful' mean?" Let me quote Jon Kabat-
Zinn in his book, *Wherever You Go, There You Are,* a
work on meditation:

"Mindfulness means paying attention in a particular way: on purpose, in the present moment, and
nonjudgmentally."

Mindfulness is about awareness, awareness of what
we are doing at any given moment. Much of the time,
we're thinking about something in the future or the
past while we perform a task. Driving or taking a
shower are good examples. We do them automatically;
they don't take much conscious thought, so we turn
our attention elsewhere. The problem arises because
we get into the habit of doing this whenever what
we're engaged in doesn't immediately and constantly
hold our attention, whether it's a conversation, a book,

or a work task. We get bored so easily. And our minds seek stimulation elsewhere.

If we do this too much, we end up spending much of our time in reliving past moments or in projections of future moments and not in being aware of the present moment. Big deal, you may say, what's wrong with that?

What's wrong is that life is made up of an ongoing series of present moments. If we're rarely aware of them, how aware are we of living? Life doesn't exist in the past or the future, but only right here, right now. Living somewhere other than the present moment can be considered a form of sleepwalking. We could walk down a street and not be aware that the sun is shining. We could have dinner with a spouse and not be listening to what they're saying (ask my wife Rebecca).

Try an experiment. Try to be present while you brush your teeth. That means not thinking of anything else during the act. It means focusing your attention solely on the act of brushing. Be aware of taste, friction, moisture, movement, etc., and only that. Notice how incredibly hard it is to maintain for even thirty seconds. Observe where your mind goes, and how it reacts ("what a stupid exercise"—a typical response when we can't do something well).

The first time I tried it, I found I could only focus my mind on the activity if I closed my eyes. Then I became aware of the taste, sound, movement, etc. I wasn't able to perform the complete brushing without my mind wandering, but I felt I did okay.

Ditto on the second morning and evening. On day three I forgot. And forgot again on days four and five. The morning of day six I "woke up" and remembered. Now I'm back to doing it "okay." For a few more days. I can see it won't last. Not enough motivation.

Here's a different way to understand the value of mindfulness:

Imagine that you're playing water volleyball at the beach. There's a lot of activity . You and your teammates are thrashing around, whipping up the water, yelling. You get the picture. Chaos. Urgency.

Imagine that you've been playing for an hour. You're tired. Bushed. Now imagine that you leave the game, pick up your scuba gear and wade into the surf.

The tiny tube feeds you air as you settle into the blue water and slowly sink into the depths. The chaos at the surface fades. There is only silence. Your body relaxes as you allow the water to support you. For as far as you can see the water is clear. How peaceful. How serene.

The volleyball game is a metaphor for our lives. We run from one activity to another. We're always striving to score one more goal, make one more point. It's tiring. Never ending. And we behave as though that's all there is. We need time outs, breaks that refresh us. That's what we get when we dive below the surface.

Going below the surface is analogous to mindfulness. There is calmness there. For a time (and it may only be a few moments) all the crazy activity ceases. We can take a deep breath and relax. The mind stops flitting to the to-do list. It stays in the present.

Are you washing a dish? Just wash the dish. It doesn't take any more time to wash it, but you're present at the washing.

Are you changing your baby's diaper? Just change the diaper.

Are you going outside to pick up the paper? Go with your mind solely on the activity. Notice how it changes the game.

How am I at this? I stink. Today I walked downstairs with an armload of dirty laundry that I had meant to deliver into the hamper upstairs. I was thinking of other things. I find it frustrating, maddening. My mind does not want to stop thinking and plotting. It continually "puts me to sleep" when I want to be awake, to be present.

I see the power and value in practicing mindfulness. I like the feeling of the deep ocean. It calms me. It helps me play the next round of volleyball with less stress.

Last week I taught a class in Sacramento. Driving home alone that evening, I stopped at a restaurant. I decided to eat my meal in a mindful manner. That is, no reading, no conversation, no stray thoughts, just totally focused on the eating.

I began to eat, looking at the food, trying to focus on its taste and smell. It was unbelievably hard. First, I caught myself reading everything in print around me— the advertising on the paper placemat, the wall posters. I would pull myself away and come back to the food.

Then I would start watching people. Oh, there's an interesting person. Oops, back to the food.

Then the food reminded me of a restaurant I loved when I was in graduate school in Norman, Oklahoma. Oops. Back to the food.

Then I started to eat fast. Had to remind myself to slow down.

Then I began to wonder how they chose the name of the restaurant. Back to the food.

Oh, what an attractive woman. Oops. Back to the food.

And on and on it went. I never focused on the food for more than five seconds at a time.

It was an eye-opening experience. I would not have

predicted that I would do so poorly at focusing on one activity. And an activity that I like, to boot. It made me wonder, am I that unfocused at all my meals? I'm afraid the answer is yes. I don't pay as much attention to my food as I think I do.

If I'm that unfocused about my food when I'm alone, what am I like when I'm with someone else? With two or three others? Amazing.

I would have done better if I had been blindfolded. I use my sight to a large degree to help distract me from whatever I'm doing. No wonder we're encouraged to close our eyes when we meditate.

One of the big payoffs for practicing mindfulness is the opportunity to recognize and give up judgments and criticisms.

One of the great stressors in our lives is our mind's amazing ability to judge people, things, actions, anything. Some of us do it more than others. But we all do it. We do it when there's no need to do it. We have a habit of doing it. A few unhappy people live their lives by it.

Here's Kabat-Zinn again:

> When you dwell in stillness, the judging mind can come through like a foghorn. I don't like the pain in my knee. . . . This is boring.. . . . I like this feeling of stillness. . . . It's not working for me. I'm no good at this. I'm no good, period. This type of thinking dominates the mind and weighs it down. It's like carrying around a suitcase full of rocks on your head. It feels good to put it down. Imagine how it might feel to suspend all your judging and instead to let each moment be just as it is, without attempting to evaluate it as "good" or "bad." This would be a true stillness, a true liberation.

A powerful exercise is to become more aware of the thoughts you have throughout the day and notice how many of them are judgments: "I like this, I don't like that." Just observe yourself. Just notice. And when we're doing our mindfulness practice, whether it's brushing our teeth or washing the dishes, notice when judgments come up and let them pass without any additional judgments ("Dang, there I go again, making a stupid judgment"). What we're working toward is making our little moments of mindfulness a judgment-free zone.

I encourage you to keep trying this exercise and to create little reminders throughout the day so you'll think of it. (That's my problem. I go unconscious to the whole thing for days at a time if I don't create little memory joggers for myself.)

Kabat-Zinn suggests this for mindfulness practice: "Try stopping, sitting down, and becoming aware of your breathing once in a while throughout the day. It can be for five minutes, or even five seconds. Let go into full acceptance of the present moment, including how you are feeling and what you perceive to be happening."

Here's the bottom line: We sometimes think it's stuff "out there" that's creating our stress. The truth is we create it by our reactions to the stuff. Just so, we can't look for the most valuable tools to relieve stress "out there." Exercise, watching our food intake, massage, vacations, all those things help and are important, but we need to look inwardly for the ultimate strategy. It's getting in touch with that ocean of calm and peace and serenity. Stop. Breathe. Relax. Be present. Ahhhhh.

10: BALANCE

The Yin and Yang of The Bamboo Forest

Aloha from Wailea, Maui, Hawaii. Rebecca and I are staying at a friend's house for a holiday. As a stress reducer, Hawaii is at the top of my list. I'm writing this on a sunny afternoon, in the back-yard, amidst a variety of exotic plants and trees. I love plants and trees with BIG leaves, and Hawaii easily provides that. A mild wind is blowing, an old cat is napping luxuriously on a bench, and a pair of black-ish-brownish birds with yellow beaks are casually combing the grassy area for insects and seeds. The swaying leaves and palm fronds create a symphony of dappled light and shade. Soft music is playing in the background. Birds sing in the trees. Is this the good life, or what?

Two days ago, Rebecca and I went on a guided hike into the Haleakala National Park. We walked through an incredible bamboo forest. We were surrounded by thousands and thousands of bamboo poles growing 30-40' tall. They grew so close together that walking through them would be impossible. We were on a plank trail cut through the forest. Bamboo crowded up to the edges. The leafy crests 40' above were so thick that the sky and sun were blotted out. It was twilight at midday. When the wind blew, the hard stalks knocked against each other, creating a percussion symphony.

It was a simple forest: nothing but green and brown

bamboo stalks, black lava rocks, and a carpet of brown and green bamboo leaves, all in deep shade.

Everyone in our group was affected by it. We stopped talking or spoke in whispers. There was a Zen-like quality to it all, as though a Japanese gardener had set it all out carefully and mindfully. It was stunning.

Later, sitting near a 200 foot high waterfall, our guide explained the dark side of the bamboo forest. Bamboo is terribly invasive. Roots run underground and continually send up tiny shoots of new bamboo. They push out or choke or overwhelm every other plant form— that's why there was nothing but bamboo for acres and acres. Bamboo is difficult to control or kill. Chop a stalk into twenty pieces and every one could take root. No one's sure, but this forest may be Chinese bamboo, which blossoms every eighty to one hundred years. Naturalists think it could bloom any time now. The fear is that the wind will spread the seeds all over the National Park and kill out the last natural forests that exist on the island.

Our guide said that the root system is so pervasive and creates such a thick interlocking mat that some people believe a bamboo forest is a single organism, rather than thousands of individual bamboos.

The walk back through the forest had a different feel. It was still beautiful and awe-inspiring, but now the twilight quality held a touch of sadness.

Once again, the yin and yang of life shows up, the light and the dark, the beautiful and the sinister. I am always struck by the amazing balance of nature that I observe and feel whenever I come to Hawaii.

In my friend's back yard, the shadows have length-ened and merged. The cat is awake, grooming itself, ready for dinner. The two yellow-beaked birds are gone. The sun is well past the yardarm, and I'm ready for a cold beer.

What is that Jimmy Buffett song? "Just another day in paradise."

You're Not the Only One

The body is a sacred garment. It's your first and last
garment; it is what you enter life in and what you
depart life with, and it should be treated with honor.
                                        —Martha Graham

I've been going to yoga classes in my neighborhood
for some time now. At first it was hard. Try squeezing your ears between your knees and you'll see
what I mean. Or lie on your back, bend your leg and
try to pull your knee into your arm pit. That particular
posture is called the "Wind Relieving Pose," for rea-
sons that become obvious when you attempt it.

I've been trying not to expect instant success
(because no matter what I expect, my body moves at its
own pace: slowly).

My body enjoys this exercise (and will drag me to
the class even when my mind doesn't want to go).
Sometimes I get into a meditative state during the
postures. Things get real quiet inside. It's nice. Nice,
that is, until someone comes in late, stands too close to
me, and invades my space. Then I shift instantly from a
blissed-out "OM" person to a resentful, angry person.

This change occurs so quickly it surprises me. Then
I feel petty and small. Come on, I say to myself, lighten
up. But I don't. I hold onto my resentment as though
it's a small, valuable coin I don't want to let go of.

Part of my flame-up might be that the intruder is
typically a 20-something woman with a model's body

who can wrap her foot behind her head while maintaining perfect balance. I'm painfully aware (in more ways than one) that I can hardly bend over without obsessing that my stiff joints are the result of age.

I also want a lot of personal space when I attempt the famous "Wind Relieving Pose."

I do not like my spiteful mood. By accident, I discovered that if I made eye contact, nodded, or spoke a friendly word, the anonymous threat turned into a normal human being, and I could let go of my hostility. Sam Keene, in his book, *Faces of the Enemy,* said that to hate someone we must keep them anonymous. Once we make them human, they are harder to hate. He's right.

At a recent class, Kent, the instructor, reminded us that people sometimes come late, not because they're lazy, but because of commitments at work and home, and that we shouldn't growl at them but instead welcome them and make space for them. Ah yes, there's the appropriate attitude, one that I wouldn't have come to by myself.

How did Kent know what I was thinking? Either I hadn't been hiding my upset very well, or I wasn't the only one who was irritated. I think it was the latter.

I'm not the only one.

These are good words to remember. Part of our stress comes from our off-base belief that we're the only one thinking/feeling whatever it is we're thinking/feeling. We all need a little gnome sitting on our shoulder, and whenever we go off on one of our weird little trips, it would whisper, "You're not the only one." That would help put things into perspective.

You're not the only one.

I am that I Am.

—Old Testament

I yam what I yam.

—Popeye

11: ART

Breathing Vincent

Beauty can pierce one like a pain.
—Thomas Mann

Rebecca and I flew to Los Angeles last week to catch the Van Gogh exhibit before it closed. I've seen a few Van Goghs over the years at various museums, but this was my first time to see so many (seventy) of his pieces at once.

The cumulative effect was that of sensing the presence of the man himself. The energy of Van Gogh was imbedded in each piece; his energy fairly leaped off the canvas. It became more intense as I moved closer to each painting. When I was only an inch away and could distinguish individual brush strokes and see the thick smears of pure color, it was almost as if I could feel the pressure with which he wielded his brush.

Knowing something about the tortured soul of the man added to my emotional experience. Here was the creative expression of a man who so desired love in his life and who felt loved by only one person in the world, his brother. Even in some of his brightly colored canvases, there seemed a sadness behind the beauty. Was it there, or did I project it onto the paintings?

Whichever it was, the final effect was the same: gut-wrenching emotional involvement.

Even now, days later, I find myself at my kitchen window, staring at the flower beds of the house next door, taking in the pinks, reds, purples, whites and yellows of the iris and roses and lilies and sage. Vincent would have wanted to paint these, I think.

Sunlight is more brilliant, more intense these days. Even my old running shoes, lying abandoned in a corner, have a certain brightness.

Once again, what shows up is the power of art to center us, to ground us, to remind us of what's important.

> If only we try to live sincerely, it will go well with us, even though we are certain to experience real sorrow and great disappointments. . . . It is good to love many things, for therein lies the true strength, and whosoever loves much performs much, and can accomplish much, and what is done in love is well done! . . . One must never let the fire go out in one's soul, but keep it burning.

> —Vincent Van Gogh, age 24.

From Paris to Snow-Chilled Beer

Life is too short to balance a checkbook.

—Howard Ogden

Part One

Rebecca and I just returned from a two-week vacation to England and France. Ah, London. Ah, Paree. It's true that travel is a major stress reliever (providing it's not a vacation from hell, where everything goes wrong. Rebecca and I did not have that type: everything went right).

We did all the touristy-kind of things and a few oddball things. A brief listing goes like this:

In England we visited

- Stonehenge, a prehistoric monument built between 3000 and 1500 BC
- Avebury, another prehistoric monument, older and bigger than Stonehenge.
- The town of Bath, where the Romans built an incredible set of temples and buildings around a hot spring. The spring still flows today and the Roman plumbing is still in operation. (And I have trouble just getting a plumber out to my house.)

In London—

- Lots of walking tours, including one focusing on the Beatles. We stood at the crosswalk where the "Abbey Road" album picture was taken. I also went on a ghost walk where I learned of supernatural doings of olde London.

- Churchill's Cabinet War Rooms. When the war ended, everybody just walked out and locked the doors and went home. The rooms became a time capsule. Very moving.
- The British Museum. The Egyptian artifacts and Greek statues were incredible.

In Paris—

- The Cathedral of Notre Dame. Amazing architecture, sculptures, and stained glass. The cathedral took hundred of years to build. I thought of all the artisans who labored on it, knowing they would never live to see it completed. That's dedication.
- The Louvre. We saw da Vinci's Mona Lisa, the Winged Victory, the Venus de Milo, statues by Michelangelo, and we had hardly begun.
- A museum of the works of Rodin. Rodin's genius was as large as his statues. He captured the triumphs and tragedies of life and love in bronze. Incredible.
- A museum (Orsay) that covers only the years 1842 to World War I. We saw paintings by Van Gogh, Renoir, Monet, and other masters whose names I can't spell.
- The catacombs. During cholera epidemics of the 16th and 17th centuries, the Paris cemeteries filled up. Officials exhumed thousands of graves and moved the bones into the catacombs, the sewer system built by the Romans. The bones are neatly piled along the sides of the passageways, which go on and on and on. The sense was of being overwhelmed by sheer

numbers. It was looking back into history, not at the architecture or art left by people, but looking at the remains of the people themselves—bakers, politicians, soldiers, children, prostitutes, doctors, carpenters, once alive and now turning to dust.

Rebecca and I had lunches of cheese, bread and fruit sitting by the Seine, wandered through lush parks, sat at sidewalk cafes sipping strong coffee and eating French pastries, took a boat ride at sunset, had sweet afternoon naps, and ate wonderful and leisurely meals. (In England, the food was good but not great, so I tried to stay on my vegetarian diet. The French food was so incredible that I ate every kind of meat, sugar and fat that I could stuff into my mouth.)

What did I take back with me from this trip? Almost everything I saw seemed a celebration of people who had a vision and the talent and energy to birth that vision, whether it was a building, a statue, a piece of stained glass, a painting, or a fine meal. With that framework, that lens, I could sit at a cafe or pub (beer in London, wine in Paris) and see a touch of what others had seen in the long circus of human existence. The great themes in all that I saw, in museum or cafe, were, not surprisingly, love, death, the beyond, and a love for the human being and the human spirit, flawed or idealized.

I was also struck by the huge tapestry of human history, from the Egyptians and the people of Stonehenge and Avebury, to a Paris street cleaner today. We're all part of this great web.

One other thing—given the great web of history stretching back 10,000 years or more, and given that individuals and groups would spend years, decades, even centuries manifesting their visions into a reality, our time on this planet is only a blink of the eye. The messages I heard over and over again as I stared at Rodin's "Thinker" or a nude by Renoir, were the old adages, "carpe diem" (seize the day), and "ars longa, vita brevis" (art is long, life is short).

How am I doing at manifesting my own vision into reality? I ask myself. How indeed.

Ah, London, ah, Paris. Definitely a stress relieving experience. Until the VISA bills come in, that is.

Part Two

Last week, with hardly enough time to wash my socks following the European trip, I went off into the Cascade Range of Oregon, camping in the Olallie Lakes area of the Mount Hood National Forest. I was in a group of five other men, including my son Alex, and two of his uncles, Robert and Ernest Herndon.

Robert and Ernest, experienced backpackers, decided that we wouldn't backpack on this trip, but would stay at a campsite with truck and van nearby. That meant that instead of eating twigs and bark, what I consider normal fare while backpacking, we ate really well, and we ate a lot. (Our reasoning was that, with all the hiking and canoeing we were doing, we needed a lot of calories. Thus we would have a breakfast of grits, venison sausage, eggs, and pancakes.) Eating the fresh trout caught from the nearby lake had us all moaning in delight.

The big surprise of the trip was the snow—there were snow banks all around, many six feet deep. This was July! Some of the higher hiking trails were completely blocked. We had our own little glacier at our campsite that came right up to the campfire. It became a handy refrigerator for storing beer and trout—just dig a hole and bury the bottle or fish.

Deer showed up in the early morning and evening, looking for a handout. Sometimes they woke us up, stomping around our tents in the predawn, stealing apples we had left in our refrigerator.

We paid a lot of attention to the wind, cloud patterns, temperature changes. I liked having a heightened awareness of the outdoors. We had good weather except for two storm fronts with lots of thunder and wind, one that skirted around us and left us dry, and another that dumped rain on us for about six hours. During part of that storm, one of the camping party, Dan, and I went out on the lake in the canoe. The lake and mountains were beautiful in the rain. I saw everything through a gray gauze. I also got soaked.

As the rain permeated my shoes and pants, I was initially annoyed by the discomfort, then remembered some writer saying that of course travel is uncomfortable; if we want to be comfortable, we should stay home. So it was fine.

Good things about camping, in addition to being closer to nature: hiking, with my mind alternating between being in the present moment, aware of smells, sounds, and sights, and being in daydream mode; climbing into a sleeping bag when exhausted; sipping smooth tequila around the campfire; lying in a hammock in the shade and thinking about how to live my life; napping in the same hammock; telling and listening to stories around the campfire; taking a lot more time for basic human functions than one would at home and not minding it; sleeping in a watertight tent in the rain; joking, sharing food, and generally being in the company of good men. Finally, taking a shower after five days of camping, and sleeping in a real bed. I wanted to make those impressions last. But they didn't.

Maybe that's why we go camping, so that we remember how good it feels to have a basic bed and shower.

I knew the trip was over when I got off the plane at San Jose and walked into the terminal and it seemed that every other person was either on a cell phone or working on a laptop, or both.

Comparing Paris to camping—in Paris, I admired art created by man; camping, I admired art created by nature. Both were incredible in their own way, but nature has the advantage: larger canvases, interactive landscapes, multi-sensory input, and smaller crowds.

John Hatt, English traveller, wrote in *The Tropical Traveller*:

> So pack your bags and go on your travels before it is too late. . . . Travel will give you a wealth of experience and pleasure which can be drawn on for the rest of your life. . . . I have rarely met anyone who regretted going on their travels. Our greatest disappointments are nearly always for what we *haven't* done—not for what we *have* done. And don't let the feeble excuse of work keep you back; remember the Haitian proverb: If work is such a good thing, how come the rich haven't grabbed it all for themselves?

12: AGING

Who's That Geezer In the Mirror?

I grow old . . . I grow old . . . I shall wear the bottoms of my trousers rolled.

—T. S. Eliot

There was an article in the paper a few weeks ago entitled, "Cosmetic Drugs Could Clear Up Skin-deep Fears of Aging." The article said that Pfizer, maker of the impotence drug, Viagra, is putting $50 million into research on "cosmeceuticals"—drugs designed to fight liver spots, hair loss and wrinkles.

The demand for these drugs "will come from the baby boomers who made Viagra so successful." The CEO of the company said: "We think these products will be worth hundreds of millions of dollars—even billions of dollars—in the marketplace."

I understand, I understand. It was a few years ago that I happened to look at my hands and thought, "My God, those are my father's hands." The wrinkles on the knuckles, the raised veins, the liver spots, that parchment look to the skin. Yeah, those are my old man's hands all right. I'd recognize them anywhere. I just didn't expect to see them on me. Or at least not so soon.

That was not a happy moment, I have to admit.

After all, my father was old. I'm not old. Okay, in years, yeah, I'm looking down the barrel of 60, but inside I'm not old. I don't feel old (except on those days when my back and hips are stiff and I understand why "old" people use canes and walkers).

I once went with a woman who told me that her father kept screaming and crying on his death bed that he wasn't old. He didn't feel old and it wasn't fair that he was dying. I understand that, too. It's easy to see the aging process in others, but we can be pretty slick about avoiding seeing it in ourselves. I've found that I can do a pretty good job at seeing a mature (but not aging) me when looking in the mirror. But I have had some heavy shocks over pictures or videotapes of myself. As they say, the camera doesn't lie. "Wow, who's that geezer? Can't be me. Please, no more pictures."

I feel the pull of contradictory forces: on the one hand, there's our society that puts so much emphasis on youth and attractiveness. Yes, I admit it, I'd like to find the fountain of youth. I like to be thought of as youthful and vigorous.

On the other hand, if we look beyond society's superficial indoctrination, we can envision a stage of life in which aging is not synonymous with "about to die." We can become an elder. Webster defines elder as "one having authority by virtue of age and experience." I like that. Being old implies uselessness; being an elder suggests alertness and vigor.

There are just two little humps we have to get over: how we handle the changes in our appearance, and how we handle the changes in our bodies as they begin to break down in little or big ways. Just two little humps.

Opposite the cosmetic drugs article was a full page

ad for a soft rubber ball about the size of a grapefruit that you tuck up under your chin and push down on. "IT WORKS LIKE A FACE LIFT WITHOUT SURGERY," the headline screamed. It promised to get rid of double chins, the "turkey-gobbler" look, sagging jaws, face wrinkles, neck and shoulder pain, and headaches. All for just $29.95.

For a fleeting moment I thought, "That would be a good price, if it worked." Then I remembered all the other crap I had bought that promised the moon for the price of a rock, and I came to my senses.

Well, sort of. I'm now thinking that I've got a ball around somewhere that's about the size of the "Profile Toner." I could easily do the exercises ("only 3 minutes a day, results in a week"). I'd have to do them in the bathroom with the door closed, though—if Rebecca caught me, there'd be some ribbing. Ah, the price of recapturing that youthful look.

The pill I would buy gladly is the one that stops hair from growing wildly in my ears. Without my vigilance, I would be walking around with big balls of white hair sticking out of my ears, long enough to braid.

Sometimes, there are good moments, like last week when I went to my local farmers' market wearing my James Dean sweatshirt. I was standing in front of the piroshki booth when the young man selling them, a Russian in his twenties, said, in a heavy accent, "Please, excuse me for asking you, but that picture on your shirt, is that of you, taken at an earlier time?"

Yes, there are good moments. But what the hell am I going to do with the $40 worth of piroshki that I bought?

Midlife Crisis? What Crisis?

There are some jokes going around the Internet called "Baby Boomers—Then and Now." Perhaps you've seen them. Here are some samples:

Then: Killer weed
Now: Weed killer

Then: Hoping for a BMW
Now: Hoping for a BM

Then: Moving to California because it's cool
Now: Moving to California because it's warm

Ah, the horrors of aging. Or is that more of a perception than a reality? In early 1999, The MacArthur Foundation Research Network on Successful Midlife Development (Whew! a long title, but it's obvious what it's about) released its findings of a ten year study of nearly 8,000 Americans: most people find the midlife years more satisfying than their younger years. The Foundation concluded that ". . . the decades between 40 and 60 are a time when people report increased feelings of well-being and a greater sense of control over many parts of their lives." Great news.

Twenty year olds have a lot more energy and firmer bodies than the typical fifty year old, certainly, but as I'm in my fifties myself, I understand now my father's muttering that, "Youth is wasted on the young." Life is indeed far richer, more joyful and fulfilling now than it ever was.

That doesn't mean everything pleases me. Boxes
are heavier than they were twenty years ago, for
instance.

One implication of the MacArthur study is that
more of us are coming to terms with the aging process.
It's not stressing us out as much as it did previous
generations who equated aging with loss of vitality
and participation in life.

When I was ten, my father's friend Ed retired. My
father worried that Ed had no other interests outside of
his job, nothing to live for. My father said that Ed
stayed in the house and watched TV. All day long. He
was dead within six months.

Today we're more apt to pick up the newspaper
and read about a great-great-grandmother, 92 years
old, earning a yellow belt in karate. (*San Francisco
Examiner*, Dec. 25, 1998)

So if you're young and stressed, take heart. The
study found that, "Both women and men, as they age,
show gains in the areas of personal autonomy and
effective management of the surrounding world. . . ."

If you consider yourself middle-aged, what's your
level of satisfaction with life compared to ten years
ago? How are you dealing with aging? Here's how
some people respond to these questions:

Claudia:
    Life just keeps getting better and better, kind
of like a fine wine. I enjoy and appreciate things
much more now. The simple pleasures are a joy
and everything has kind of mellowed.

Rene:
    I'm now 51, and life is good. My children are
grown, on their own, and they have given me

eight grandchildren. I am constantly reminded of the saying, "being a grandmother is God's way of giving you a second chance at being a good mother." It's so true. I have more patience with the grandkids than I did raising my children. This is the best part of getting older.

One of the hardest things about getting older is losing your parents. I lost my Mom in 1992 and my Dad a year later (almost to the day). Taking care of them in the last days was unbelievably hard. This was the worst part of getting older.

Daniel:

Yes, I consider myself middle-aged. I find that things don't bother me as much as they used to. I eliminate stress wherever possible. For example, when I was younger I used to see relatives because it was proper. Now I refuse to be put in that situation. If I do go to visit and things start getting stressful, I leave! I am not rude and I do not explain, I just leave (and feel much better for doing so).

I find I am doing more and enjoying it more. Some of it is because I learned to please myself first, and my child is grown and on his own.

Life is great! I think, in my case, my attitudes changed.

Norma:

I'm 66 and retired for 10 years. I was a career woman and have never NOT worked. I was glad to have freedom from the clock after forty years, and I did work my way up the corporate ladder and I know what management stress is.

Now I wonder how I ever found time to

work! Retirement is exactly what you make it, and enjoying it is a direct reflection of your attitude about it.

For me, I love it! I can do anything I want at any time I want. The trick is to stay healthy, and there is a lot you can do for yourself. The next trick is to get involved in the activities that you always wanted to do but never had the time.

I love being retired and encourage everyone to plan for it psychologically, financially and emotionally. You must believe you've earned it to enjoy it!

Patrice:

At 37 1/2 years old (midlife yet?) I am much happier than before.

I have a moral code and a belief system in place, whereas before I didn't know how I felt about most things.

I have a spiritual base, a belief and reliance on God that comforts me when I need it and gives me joy all other times.

I am a much better parent because I know where I stand on issues, and I am able to guide my children with confidence.

My marriage (2nd one!) is stable, happy and based on mutual beliefs, values and passions. I am old enough and wise enough (been there!) to know that there are frumpy times in every marriage and that to seek happiness elsewhere is not the answer and is only asking for a new set of problems.

I laugh more and sweat the small stuff less.

In short, I like me better and can only imagine myself getting better with time!

Reggie:

Well, I'm almost 47 and I don't feel middle aged. Yes, my body has more aches and pains. My spare tire is expanding slowly but surely, and I can't read anything without removing my glasses first. But I'm more excited about living than ever before. I feel at the top of my game. I am more creative than I've ever been. People are getting great results from the work I do for them. If this is middle age, I'll take another 30 or 40 years of it.

Terri:

I'm going through a midlife crisis, or something akin to it, midlife burnout! Both my husband and I read the statistics and saw the report of the Mac Arthur Foundation Research on Midlife Development on the news. Both of us said that that doesn't reflect what we are going through. Both of us feel as if we won't make it to retirement; we are so tired and burned out with our jobs, where we live, etc.

I'm turning 50 and my husband is turning 53. He's a plumber, which is physically demanding work. After years, his body is complaining. He wants out! I'm a senior buyer of electronics. It is an extremely stressful, ten hours a day or more, thankless job. I want out! Trouble is, I actually make more than my husband. I want to change careers, but I feel as if it is too late. I can't afford to take a big cut in pay and don't have the energy or time to take classes at night. We are both trapped. The only saving grace is that we have a gym here at work. I work out every day, which keeps me sane. Trouble is, I'm in pain every day.

I'm afraid I may have to give up my workout, which terrifies me.

My mother is elderly and living in a care facility. We need to be close to her. We take the one hour drive every Saturday or Sunday and spend the day with her. It is physically, spiritually and emotionally draining. When I get home I feel hysterical. I usually have insomnia that night. I have to fight the urge to get drunk or eat myself into oblivion. My father is gone. My husband's father is dying of cancer in Texas. Luckily he has a brother and a sister still living in Texas. We are worried about his mother.

I had to break my mother's heart yesterday and tell her that we are not going to spend Easter with her. We are going to Southern California to spend Easter with my daughter. We tried travelling with my Mom when my daughter graduated from college. It was awful. I won't go into the gory details, but let's just say there aren't enough bathrooms along the way. My husband said he will never travel with her again. I feel as if I'm caught in the middle, having to choose who I should be loyal to.

This is the grand Middle Age?

Part of the reason, I think, I feel so hysterical when I get home after being with my mother for a day, is that I'm afraid this will be me in a few years. Who's going to change my diapers and cut my toenails? I don't want to live that way! The only other alternative is death, and I'm not ready for that one either. My mother was always a rock. Ran the house with an iron will and an iron fist. I can't stand seeing her this way.

Needless to say, I have no time for myself. I

don't have time to read or reflect or do any of those things that make life bearable. I don't have time to go to church, which makes me feel very guilty. I'm not sure that God understands. I know He wants me to put Him first and go to church. I'm not sure where God is on the long list of priorities in my life. About the only time I pray is when I am driving to work, unless my mind is so full I can't even pray. I'm a pretty poor example of a Christian. Because I'm so stressed, I tend to lose my temper much too quickly.

Now that I have thoroughly depressed you, I guess I had better get back to work. I feel better, just being able to get some of this off my chest.

Natalie:

I turn 49 this week, so I'm in my midlife. I love my life. Each year gets better and better. On Christmas Day I made a list of 42 goals that I want to achieve by my 50th birthday. I'm still working on the list to get it up to 50. This is an exciting time for me, and I'm spending time and energy to create my future. I intend to be in the best physical, spiritual, financial and relationship shape I have ever been in when I turn 50!

As I grow older I love my life, and especially myself, better and better. Life seems to be getting easier since I'm going with the flow of life, rather than trying to battle the current.

I take each day as a special gift from God and look for the beauty in it. Even on the lonely, sad, empty days, I know I'm in my right place, doing my right work in life. And I know the emptiness or whatever the feeling might be will pass. This is one of the greatest gifts of aging—knowing deep within my soul that "this too shall pass."

So I embrace life and look forward to the next 50 years. I believe they will be even better than the first 50. Look at all the wisdom I get to make good use of!

When I was 32, I was in graduate school for psychology. We were all working adults in our 30s-50s. They split the class into two sections, under 40 and over 40. I was very embarrased for the "over 40s" and felt bad for them being old. Our task was to discuss our lives. We "under 40s" were very serious, talking about finding meaning in our lives and our search for truth. Very serious and sincere. I noticed, however, that the "over 40s" were laughing in the other room. What was there to laugh about? Life is serious in your 30s. When we got back together, they talked about how they had let go of the search and were now enjoying life more, loving themselves more, and accepting life as it was. They were still changing. It was just easier for them going with the flow of life. I decided then and there—I can't wait to turn 40!

Each decade gets richer and I enjoy the fullness of life more and more.

Living life is a good thing!

Jamie:

I am now entering my midlife. Here are some things that help me cope with stress today compared to ten years ago.

I have two young children ages four and eight, both girls. Most people think that children are the cause of stress. However, I look at it differently. I look at my children as blessings and wish I were them and living the carefree life they have currently as we, their, parents, are constantly looking out for their needs. Every weekend, I spend about an hour with the girls in the morning just tumbling in the bed, giggling, laughing and planning the day. Most families these days rarely talk to their children.

I read somewhere that to keep a healthy heart, read a comic strip daily, as laughter is the best medicine. I also watch cartoons with my kids, as it makes me laugh, and my girls know I am with them. I also sit down and watch my fish in the fish tank occasionally, as I also read somewhere that watching fish can be a soothing method to relax and relieve tension. I heard in a recent study that people who have pets also have a higher life expectancy.

Most of all, if I am in a stressful situation, I take that deep breath, stop, think about what I am doing, and usually tell myself, I'm not going to die if I don't get it done right away. Even stepping away from the situation for 30 minutes usually alleviates the stress. By then, I can usually gather my thoughts and proceed without difficulty.

To close, here's a few more "Baby Boomers—Then and Now" jokes.

Then: Long hair
Now: Longing for hair

Then: You're growing pot
Now: Your growing pot

Then: Trying to look like Marlon Brando or Elizabeth Taylor

Now: Trying not to look like Marlon Brando or
Elizabeth Taylor

Then: Seeds and stems
Now: Roughage

If I had known
I was going to
live this long, I
would have
taken better
care of myself.

—Eubey Blake

It is so easy to stand frozen by
our fear of being thought foolish.

—Mary Hamilton

Fear is something you have to
throw in a corner. Constantly.
Beacause it never goes away.

—F. Lee Bailey

Where there's fear there's power.

—Starhawk

13: SEEKING HELP

Mark McGwire, A Very Classy Guy
September, 1998

By now you've either had your fill of the media coverage of Mark McGwire's record breaking home runs or it didn't interest you at all.

I'm not going to talk about the record he set with his 62nd home run (which I saw on TV; it brought tears to my eyes) or how classy he's been in handling the whole media circus around him (which he has).

Instead, I want to tell you about an earlier time in his life when things weren't going so well. Mark came into the majors in 1987 and had a great rookie season, including his unanimous selection as rookie of the year. But the next four years were a downward slide to hell. His marriage broke up, and he worried about his absence in his young son's life. The divorce was painful, and the pain lingered; subsequent relationships with women seemed to make things worse.

Bud Geracie, in a September 4 article in the *San Jose Mercury News*, said of McGwire: "He'd grown up with certain ideals about how a life should be led, and he'd been leading that life just a few fast years back. Now he was lost." To add to his misery, the 1991 season was his worst as a ballplayer. His batting average for the year was an embarrassing .201. His agent said "Everything that could go wrong did go wrong."

At the end of that season, Mark began seeing a psychotherapist. Looking back, he said in an interview:

I was a stupid, young, immature kid. If I could go back, knowing the things I know now, the person I am now, there is no question in my mind the marriage would have worked. . . .

I wish I could sit here and say we worked for it. We tried. But I didn't know myself. One thing I've learned in therapy, if you don't know yourself, if you don't like yourself, you're never going to be good to anybody if you can't be good to yourself. And that's where I am now.

That's why I say things happen for a reason. Too bad I had to go through a divorce to do the things I needed to do.

McGwire still sees his psychotherapist. "We talk all the time," he said. "It's a lifetime thing."

That was smart of McGwire to seek professional help when he had reached the edge of his own resources. And incredible of him to be so open about it in an interview. He's not ashamed of having sought help. And of still getting help.

Imagine what direction his career might have taken had he tried to tough it out as so many people do. "I don't need help," many snarl, "I can do it on my own." How many people with great potential have failed to reach it because they were too proud, too ego-involved to admit they couldn't handle their problems by themselves?

In a TV interview, McGwire said, "The bottom line is, we control our own destiny by swinging the bat." Whether it's at the plate or by seeking professional help.

Yeah, McGwire is a classy guy. A very classy guy.

"Let's Begin, Shall We?"

For almost a year now, Lou my barber, has been telling me about the HBO gangster series, "The Sopranos."

"It's great, you gotta see it," he tells me.

"Lou, I don't get HBO," I complain.

He ignores me and tells me about the show: "This Tony Soprano is a mobster see, he's a mafioso in New Jersey, he's about forty, with a wife and two kids." (Another television attempt to capture the mythology of *The Godfather* films, I think. Spare me.)

Lou goes on: "So Tony collapses from panic attacks caused by stress, and his doctor sends him to a psychiatrist."

"A psychiatrist?" I snort. "Is this like the movie, *Analyze This*?"

"Well, it's funny at times, and I laugh watching this guy squirm in the shrink's office, but no, it's not a comedy," Lou says, struggling to find shape in my hayfield of hair.

"Well, I don't get HBO," I say again, to end the discussion.

Last week I was in a motel room in Sacramento and it happened to be the night that the series was being rerun, starting with the original episode. I decided to watch it.

Wow.

Good script, good acting, lots of layers of meaning, well done, but the "wow" came from watching Tony Soprano, gangster boss, going to see a shrink. He doesn't want to be there, yet he wants to know why he's collapsing with pains in his chest. He walks out of one session, he doesn't show for another, but he keeps coming back. He wants to understand himself in spite of himself.

There's a good scene where Tony takes his wife out to dinner to tell her his secret, that he's seeing a psychiatrist. He's not sure she won't make fun of him for it. She's thrilled.

Wow. My image of how TV handles therapists is the old Bob Newhart show, where it's all played for laughs and no viewer would ever think of actually going to a psychiatrist after watching the ineffectual, bumbling Newhart.

This is different. Tony is a regular guy, an everyman, someone we can relate to on many levels— troubles at home with wife and kids, troubles with co-workers, business politics, an aging mother, etc. (Okay, he's a mobster boss, so he isn't *exactly* like us, but that's not the point.)

The point is that the psychiatrist is portrayed as someone who can help us understand the pain in our lives.

I'm big on getting professional help for understanding ourselves and our pain because I've gotten help for myself at important times in my life: when my first marriage was unraveling (therapy didn't save it, but my wife and I got great guidance in making the divorce less traumatic for our then four–year–old son); when I moved to California and felt cut loose and adrift, without purpose; when my son became a teenager and had to work through his own demons; when my second wife and I couldn't agree on whether to start a family. Getting help allows us to see options we couldn't see before.

I hope "The Sopranos" helps to create an image of

psychiatry that will encourage a lot of people who ordinarily wouldn't ever go to a shrink ("I can work out my own problems, I don't need anyone giving me advice.") to reconsider.

And now I'm hooked on "The Sopranos" after only one episode. Lou was right. Now either I've got to buy HBO or grovel to get my HBO-subscribing friends to record the shows for me.

The true value of a human being can be found in the degree to which he has attained liberation from the self.

—Albert Einstein

It is never too late
to be what you
might have been.

—George Eliot

14: NOSTALGIA

Nostalgia Ain't What It Used to Be

Nostalgia- 1: the state of being homesick 2: a wistful or excessively sentimental yearning for return to or of some past period or irrevocable condition.

—Webster's Collegiate Dictionary

You might associate nostalgia more with day dreaming and wasting time than with stress relief, but when I led stress workshops for the Meyer Friedman Institute, an important exercise was to spend five minutes remembering positive past events. The idea is that recalling pleasurable memories gives us a little break from the pressure cooker of our daily lives.

If you're over 35, Roy Rogers' death, in July of 1998, may have triggered some nostalgia in you. Did you have a Roy Rogers lunch box? Can you sing a stanza of "Happy Trails To You"?

I remember Roy Rogers coloring books and comic books and his TV show. When I put on my cowboy hat, my bandanna (rolled, tied around the neck with the knot at the side—I never knew its function, but it sure looked cool), and strapped on my six-guns, I *was* Roy Rogers.

When I was ten, Roy came to town. My folks took

me to see him at Madison Square Garden on a Sunday afternoon. I was decked out in my complete cowboy outfit. I'd have worn spurs and chaps if I'd had them.

Our seats were high up in the stands, so when Roy trotted out on Trigger to the cheers of thousands of kids, he was very small and far away. No matter. There was my hero, in the flesh. Roy Rogers. I jumped up and down with excitement. (I was able to do this without my six-guns flapping stupidly against my legs because I borrowed a little trick from Roy and tied the holsters to my legs with string. Sure, Roy used rawhide leather thongs to stabilize his holsters, but string worked.)

After Roy said hello to all of us junior cowpokes, he asked the kids who'd gone to Sunday School that morning to stand up. I watched in horror as almost every kid (it seemed to me) in the Garden stood up and cheered again.

I didn't go to Sunday School. My parents hardly ever went to church.

I couldn't stand up and be counted in Roy's army of little soldiers. Roy had no use for me. I slumped in my seat, defeated.

For a long time after, I wondered if Roy would ever forgive me.

Ah Yes, I Remember It Well

I t's nice to reflect on those aspects of the holiday season that make all the madness and preparation worthwhile: family, closeness, spiritual awareness, a sense of peacefulness and love, and memories.

Ah, memories.

One of the nice ways that we can take time to pause and relax is when we hear a holiday song that has special significance for us. It may be the song itself, or it may be a particular recording. From Bing Crosby and Frank Sinatra to Elvis and Willie Nelson, holiday songs can conjure up vivid memories.

For me, a special song is Irving Berlin's classic, *White Christmas*, recorded by Clyde McPhatter and The Drifters in 1954. It was the first 45 record I ever bought. I remember going to a little record store on 14th St., off Union Square in Manhattan on a dark, snowy afternoon. I was 13.

You can't mistake The Drifters' version for anyone else's—it has a real doo wop arrangement ("I, I, I, I'm dreaming of a white Christmas"). Every time I hear it, I sing along, remembering another era, another time—and smile.

Another memory song for me is Bobby Helms' *Jingle Bell Rock*. I associate it with the winter of my freshman year at Albany State University. I lived in a dormitory, one of four that formed a square with a grassy quadrangle in the middle. On a weekday evening shortly before Christmas break, snow began to fall. I opened my window and looked out over the quad. It was beautiful, the snow falling silently through a light sky. I noticed that not many others were appreciating this winter wonderland, so I put my record player in the window and played *Jingle Bell Rock* at full blast. Windows in the other dorms flew open and hundreds of students looked out, many waving, some shouting and singing.

It wasn't long before the dorm counselor showed up, telling me to knock it off. It was too bad. The next song I'd planned to play was The Drifters' *White Christmas*.

Now, whenever I hear Bobby Helms, I can see the snow falling in the quadrangle. It's very peaceful, very joyful.

Whether it's a sacred carol or rock'n roll, music is an important part of the holiday season.

Happy Holidays/Joyeux Noel/Feliz Navidad/God Jul/Buon Natale.

15: FORGIVENESS

Letting Go

My aunt got angry at her sister's husband for some major indiscretion. She didn't talk to him for years. I never asked her about it, but I can imagine the satisfaction she got from nursing that grudge day after day.

I know how enjoyable it can be to hold a grudge. I can relive the erroneous deed over and over in my mind. Part of what feels so good is the self-righteousness.

I know I'm right. And they're wrong. Or stupid or both. They made a big mistake. I'm right. No doubt about it. I'm hurt, I'm angry. They've done something terrible to me. So I nurse the hurt and hold tight to my righteousness.

As long as I keep it to myself, that is. I may get confirmation for my grudge from friends the first few times I air it, but if I keep it up, my friends say, "Are you still holding on to that? Isn't it time to give it up?"

So grudges are best kept secret, in the dark, where they can grow like mushrooms.

Grudges, based on our judgments (this is wrong, that is right), are easier to nurture than they are to let go. Once we hatch one, it sticks to us. It loves to be paid attention to, to be stroked and talked to.

To let go of a grudge is to forgive. Laurence Sterne said, "Only the brave know how to forgive. . . . A coward never forgave; it is not in his nature."

It takes maturity to forgive. A child finds it hard to forgive. The child in the adult finds it hard to forgive.

Some say forgiveness is the activity of love. I like that.

And it's not as though we have only one chance. We get lots and lots of opportunities; strangers and loved ones are always providing us with rich experiences that we judge as right/wrong, that we get upset over because they did it to us, and that we have the opportunity to forgive, to "get off it."

As the question goes, would you rather be right or be happy?

You're probably familiar with the Zen tale of the two monks who came upon an attractive young woman standing beside a rain-swollen gutter, unable to cross. One monk picked her up and carried her across the street. He put her down and the monks continued on their way. After two hours of walking in silence, the second monk said, "My brother, I am disturbed. It's a rule of our order that we not touch a woman, and you violated that rule."

The first monk laughed. "Are you still carrying that woman? I put her down hours ago."

What are we carrying that we can't put down? Isn't it getting heavy? Who can we forgive?

While we're at it, let's start with forgiving ourselves.

16: OUR SHADOW SIDE

"The Wolf of Gubio"
A Story of St. Francis

Gubio is a small city in Italy, close to Assisi, where St. Francis was born and grew up. In those days, the people of Gubio were proud of their city and of themselves. When they would travel and someone would ask, "Where are you from?" they would say, with great pleasure, "I? I am from Gubio."

Once the city of Gubio was in a great deal of trouble. A townsperson was found dead on the streets one morning. He was partly devoured. People were horrified.

A few nights later, another person was murdered in a similar fashion. A woman claimed she was looking out her window and had seen the shadow of a giant wolf.

The town panicked. People barred their doors and did not go out after sundown. Police walked the streets in pairs, but one night two policemen were killed together. The citizens demanded that their mayor do something.

The mayor had heard of a holy man in the next town, Assisi, who was reputed to be able to talk to animals.

"Have him come and talk to the wolf," a councilman shouted. "Have him tell the wolf to go away."

"Yes," said another, "tell the wolf to go to some other town."

So the mayor sent a delegation to Assisi. At the town's piazza, the gentlemen asked for the holy man who could talk to animals. A young boy pointed out Francis, who was talking to people at a corner of the piazza.

"Him? He's dressed in rags. He looks like a beggar, not a holy man."

They approached Francis anyway, and explained their situation. "You must come and help us."

Francis agreed to come.

A few days later, the people of Gubio saw a small man walk into the forest at the edge of their city. "That's St. Francis," someone said. They crossed themselves; this holy man would surely be devoured by the wolf.

At sundown, Francis emerged from the forest with a huge gray wolf at his side. The wolf was indeed a giant. The two walked to the piazza. Word spread quickly and everyone rushed to the piazza to see the wolf and hear the holy man banish it. Or perhaps he would let them kill it.

Francis raised his hand for silence. Then he spoke. "The wolf will not harm you any more," he shouted.

The townspeople roared their approval. He raised his hand again and the crowd quieted.

"But," he said, and he paused, "you must feed your wolf."

The townspeople did not roar. They fell silent. Francis turned and walked the wolf back to the forest, then started back down the road to Assisi. He disappeared into the dusk.

The people were upset, angry. "What did he mean, feed our wolf?" "It's not our wolf." "We should have killed it when we had the chance." "The holy man is crazy." "He was no help at all," and so on.

That night, all doors were barred again and no one dared go out on the streets.

One little girl, who had been in the piazza, asked for large helpings at the dinner table and secretly dropped the food into her apron. Later, she put it all on a plate and, trembling, afraid the wolf might be waiting right outside, opened the front door and put the plate of food on the step. In the morning, the food was gone.

She told her friends what she had done. The next night, many children put plates of food out for the wolf. At first the adults were angry. "We should be poisoning the wolf, not wasting good food on it." But when weeks went by and they noticed that no policemen or soldiers were killed on patrol at night, they had to agree that the children were right. They set up a rotation among families so that food would be put out for the wolf every night.

The killings stopped. People went out of their houses again without fear.

In time, word about their feeding the giant wolf got around. When they would travel, and someone would ask them, "Where are you from?" and they would answer, "I am from Gubio," the person would say, "Gubio? Don't you have a wolf?" and they would say with pride, "Yes, we have a wolf."

Years went by, and finally the wolf grew old and died. The townspeople buried him with a great ceremony and many flowers.

And a lament rose up from the people of Gubio, and they cried, "How shall we now feed our wolf?"

One way to interpret this story is to think of the

wolf as our fears, or as those parts of our personality that we don't like, won't acknowledge, want to keep hidden away. Carl Jung, the noted psychologist, called this aspect of ourselves the shadow. We put parts of ourselves that we wish to keep hidden in our shadow. Interestingly, *positive* aspects of ourselves that we don't want to acknowledge also go into the shadow.

Denying our shadow doesn't make it go away. It's part of us, like it or not. When we deny our shadow, it leaks out, usually in the form of projection onto other people. Once, years ago, when I was ragging about someone else's shortcomings, a friend said to me, "You know, what you don't like in others is often what you don't like in yourself." He was speaking of my shadow, my wolf.

Positive aspects of ourselves kept in the shadow can take the form of excessive admiration or hero-worship. When I was in high school, I worshipped James Dean, the actor. He was everything I wanted to be—sexy, brooding, sensitive, intense. Rather than explore or develop those aspects in myself, I chose to see myself in Dean. It was easier, safer. It's like saying. "I want to be a painter, but I could never be a Van Gogh, so why bother? Instead, I'll admire what he accomplished and never pick up a brush."

The Rabbi Zuzya once said, "When I die and meet God, He will not say to me, 'Why were you not Moses?' Instead, He will say, 'Why were you not Zuzya?'"

To be complete, we must acknowledge our shadow side. We need to own it. We need to do the work to accept all parts of ourselves, the good, the bad, the ugly. That's feeding our wolf. By doing so, the wolf doesn't go away, but it does stop eating at us, gnawing away at our confidence, our power, our ability .

17: HUMOR

"Take My Wife—Please."

I joked about every prominent man in my lifetime, but never met one I didn't like.

—Will Rogers

Henny Youngman, comedian, "King of the One-Liners," died on February 24, 1998. He died of pneumonia that developed after he came down with a cold while doing two shows a night for a week in San Francisco. He was 91! Two shows a night at 91? Amazing. He had to have loved his work. I doubt that he did it to pay the mortgage.

Laughter must make you live longer. Sure, look at George Burns.

His more than six decades as a working comic made me think:

Blessed are the comedians, for they help us to take ourselves less seriously.

Blessed are the comedians, for they know the value of laughter.

Blessed are the comedians, for they give us perspective on our problems.

Who in your life makes you laugh? A co-worker, a friend, a son or daughter? Cherish them, be grateful for them. They help relieve your stress. They help keep you young.

I'm lucky. I have two people who make me laugh a lot, my wife, Rebecca, and my friend, Barry. When my son, Alex, was a little boy, he kept me laughing *all* the time.

As much as I love people who make me laugh, I love to make people laugh. I remember how proud I was, as a boy, when I could make my mother laugh. I wanted to erase the clouds of anger and depression that sometimes surrounded her.

Blessed are the comedians, for they see the world with a different, perhaps twisted, viewpoint that surprises us.

Blessed are the comedians, for they help us lighten up.

"Take my wife—please."

18: LOSS

There Are Giants Leaving This Land
April, 1999

I can't go on.
You must go on.
I'll go on.

—Samuel Beckett

I n the spring of 1999, three giants in professional
sports retired: Michael Jordan, basketball;
Wayne Gretzky, hockey; and John Elway, football.
Sports fans around the country were in mourning. I
know how they felt. I've just lost two giants in my life.

The ministers at my Unity church have left, having
"played their last game" this past Sunday. Stan
Hampson was the minister for the last seventeen years.
I started attending about six years ago. In that time, he
became my spiritual teacher.

A few years ago Stan met Susan Burnett, another
Unity minister. They married, and are now Stan and
Susan Burnett-Hampson. Susan became an associate
minister. I related to her immediately. I was overjoyed.
Now I had two spiritual teachers.

And now they're leaving.

Stan's last lesson was about the joy of friendship.
He talked about how hello and goodbye are two sides

of the same coin.

He told a folk tale of a desert wanderer who heard the voice of Allah telling him to go to a certain oasis and fill his pockets with pebbles. "Then go to sleep," Allah commanded, "and in the morning you will be both happy and sad."

In the morning, the man discovered that the pebbles had been turned into rare jewels. He was happy about his good fortune, but sad that he had left so many pebbles behind.

Stan encouraged us to think of the gems we have, not the ones we might have had.

"The loving is worth the crying," he said. Love is elastic, expansive, always growing. The crying deepens the loving.

He asked us to be open to new gems that we would discover. "Every relationship has a farewell built into it," he said.

And then he was done. The service was over. I hurt. I wasn't ready for my superstar to leave the game.

In the courtyard, I stood in line to say good-bye to Stan and Susan. A man I knew turned to me and asked, "How are you?" I told him I was sad and hurting. Then I made my fatal mistake: I asked him how he was.

"I'M GREAT!" he shouted. "I'M TERRIFIC! THERE'S NO REASON TO BE SAD. I HAVE THEM HERE." He tapped himself on his chest. "AND I CAN TALK TO THEM ANYTIME I WANT. I DON'T HAVE TO STAND IN LINE."

I knew what he meant, but excuse me, Mr. Sunshine, I want to be with my grief right now. My sadness is an expression of my love, and I don't want any suggestion to the contrary.

I went home and did hard physical labor through the afternoon, which is the best way I have of dealing

with sadness and grief. I carted dozens of wheelbar-
rows of mushroom compost a few hundred yards to
my newly-created raised beds. I carried a lot of emotional baggage, too.

Now my back and arms are tired, my hands are
chapped, and I can tap my chest and think, "Yes, Stan
and Susan are in here, and I hear their message." It's
about love. That's all it's about. That's all it was ever
about. How deeply can we learn to love?

Jordan and Gretzky and Elway have played their
last game. Stan and Susan haven't retired, but they've
played their last game at this church. Giants all. And
weren't we lucky to have either seen these giants win
the game in the final seconds, or to have heard them
say words that pierced our hearts.

When you know what you want and you want it badly enough, you'll find a way to get it.

—Jim Rohn

19: PROCRASTINATION

Honing an Old Familiar Art

procrastination is the
art of keeping
up with yesterday
— Don Marquis

Never do today what you can put off till tomorrow.
— Matthew Browne

Do you put things on your "to do" list and keep transferring them to new lists on down through the ages so that you're still faced with "clean out garage" five years later?

You know, this is not good stress management. Continually seeing that little reminder of a task undone can create uneasy feelings of guilt and inadequacy. Best to throw the entire list away. Out of sight, out of mind.

Second best would be if your garage collapsed in a strong wind or burned to the ground. As you stood in front of the shambles or ashes, you could be thankful you didn't waste a precious afternoon cleaning it out.

During one long period of my life, procrastination was my friend and companion, my drinking buddy. I don't like to think of the missed opportunities and fractured relationships that it caused. I'm past a lot of it now. Not completely, of course. Some relationships are hard to break off completely.

Here are some principles I've learned:

1. Do the dreaded thing with someone else, not alone. My wife wanted us to clean out the garage. I was able to deftly put if off for some time, but finally I got tired myself of wading through layers of junk, searching for something I couldn't find. We circled a Sunday afternoon on the calendar and I geared myself up, atti- tude-wise, that this would be worth the effort. It turned out to be not as long or as difficult as I expected, and the clean, spacious garage was a joy to behold. We even joked about eating dinner out there. All that's left is a pile of stuff in a corner of the back yard waiting to go to Good Will. It's been there for weeks now. Yes, I said I'd cart it off. Yes, it's an eyesore, but I look beyond it into the squeaky-clean garage. I'll get around to doing it. Really.

2. Arrange it so someone else is depending on you. I had been meaning to clean out my clothes closet for so long I was afraid those striped bell bottoms from the '70s might come back into fashion before I could get rid of them. Every time I opened my closet, I was reminded of what the organization experts are fond of say- ing: "The clutter in your closet reflects the clutter in your life. Clean up one and you'll clean up the other." Still, I did nothing

   Then, a few weeks ago a local charity called and asked if I had any clothes to contribute.

Their truck would be on my block in a few days. "Yes," I shouted, "come by. I'll have some clothes." I didn't get around to doing anything until an hour before the truck was due, but then I took a deep breath and plunged in. In thirty minutes I had big piles of clothes out on the porch. It felt great. So far, I've only regretted throwing out one pair of pants. Not a bad ratio. I'm now waiting for the rest of my life to reflect the pristine organization of my closet.

3. Allow guilt to consume you. My wife and I spent a weekend with my brother, Don, and his wife at their summer cottage. We had a great time. From the day we returned I planned to call Don to thank him. It didn't happen. Then I started putting it on my "to do" list: CALL DON. Weeks went by. "What if he calls me first," I thought, "then I'll really feel bad. Must call him first." CALL DON. More weeks went by. Finally I couldn't stand it any longer. I called him and apologized for taking so many months to thank him for his hospitality. "Months?" he asked. I looked at the calendar. It had been not quite three weeks. Guilt, I love it. It's such an exquisite form of torture.

Those are a few tips on breaking the icy grip of procrastination. If they don't work, remember Scarlett O'Hara's words at the close of *Gone With the Wind*: "After all, tomorrow is another day."

I was going to clean out the basement today but both the Giants and 49ers are on TV. Could be some good games.

Sitting in the Dugout

I t's bad enough striking out, but when we don't even step up to the plate and take a swing, we can't call ourselves players. We're either on the field or in the stands.

End of the year: time to pause and look back at the past year and forward to the future. It's a time to be aware of any nagging little behaviors that get in the way of our forward momentum. How do we want to be different?

I had a reminder this week that one of my nagging little behaviors is procrastination.

A few months ago, Rebecca said that she had mentioned me to an editor she knew. Rebecca told her that I would send her some of my columns for consideration. It seemed like a good opportunity for me.

Yet, I kept putting it off. Weeks went by. At first, I told myself that I was too busy to get to it right now. Then I forgot about it.

After a month, Rebecca asked me if I had written to the editor. Feeling guilty, I finally sent off some articles.

Right after Christmas, Rebecca heard from the editor who said that she had hired someone to write stress management articles just a week before she received mine.

That stung. I was embarrassed, shamefaced. Might I have gotten the assignment? I'll never know.

I sat with that one for awhile, trying to pinpoint the root of this particular self-destructive behavior of mine that surfaces every so often. Then I shifted to plans to keep this from happening again. I'm tired of missing opportunities. How do I want to be different next year? How will my decision play out in my actions? What am I committed to doing every single day?

I remember Tony Robbins saying, "It is in your moments of decision that your destiny is shaped." We've all made decisions in the past that were only half-hearted, that we didn't really mean to keep. These shape our destiny as much as the "I'll do it no matter what" kind.

Wouldn't you know it, I had lunch with an old friend, Ken, soon afterward, and he casually mentioned that he'd read that most people are committed to very few things in their lifetime. That led to a discussion of what we've been truly committed to in our lives. What a depressing conversation.

Today, as I stand at the threshold of my future, I have the opportunity to step up to the plate and take some swings to stop an old unwanted behavior.

So do you.

The aim of life is to live,
and to live means to be
aware, joyously, drunkenly,
serenely, divinely aware.

—Henry Miller

20: TIME

Hello/Goodbye Saturday

I had dinner with a friend the other night, a friend who has a stressful job. She said that some days she really wonders if she fits in. She debates whether her talents are appreciated, whether she should stay, the all-too-common cry of today's worker.

Then she brightened. "But I have my weekends." She explained that her greatest stress reliever is unstructured time. "Time to myself, where there's nothing I have to do, no place I have to be." She even hesitates to make plans with a friend to go to a movie. "Let's play it by ear" is a favorite expression of hers on the weekends.

The same day we had dinner, the *San Jose Mercury News* (August 5, 1999) ran an article on the front page entitled "Saturdays Becoming Frantic, Not Fun." It compared the Saturdays of the past ("a day of leisure, . . . mornings in bed and afternoons lolygagging in a hammock") to Saturdays of today ("a massive attack of errands, perpetual soccer games, and hard-core SUV mileage. The weekend has been slashed from two days to one."). I've been feeling that way myself, and I don't even have any children at home. But one trip to the dry cleaners and supermarket, mow the lawn and water the garden and bingo, there goes Saturday.

It was while I was resting in a hammock at a campsite in Oregon a few weeks ago that I thought I wanted more of my Saturdays back. More unstructured time. I'm starting to switch some of the weekend chores to weekdays. It isn't as easy as I thought. I'm a creature of habit. For example, I've gone food shopping on Saturday or Sunday for as long as I can remember. Do I dare shop on a Monday? Do I dare disturb the universe?

I have been able to move mowing the lawn off the weekend dance card. That wasn't too hard. But food shopping. I hear the siren call of Safeway: Come to me now.

It's worth the fight. This Saturday afternoon I took a nap during the time I would normally mow. Wonderful. Sheer bliss.

I remember when I was a kid, and Saturday was my favorite day of the week. Time to myself. Unstructured time. Time to read, to play, to hang out, to, dare I say it, waste. These days, wasting time is close to sacrilege.

My refrigerator is almost empty. Should I shop today, Sunday, or do without for one more day? I'd like to go for a hike. Let's see, shop or hike? Hike or shop? Feed the belly or feed the soul?

This one is a no-brainer.

21: SUCCESS

"The Musician of Taguang"
A Burmese Folktale

I'm sure you've heard the statement, "God, grant me patience and give it to me right now." The same can be said for success; we have a tendency to be impatient around it.

Here's an interesting folktale on that topic.

A long time ago, in the town of Tagaung, there lived a couple who had one son. His name was Maung Pon. As the boy grew into adolescence, his father thought he should have a profession.

"Our family has never had a musician," the father mused. "That's not right. Maung Pon will be a musician. He will become a great harp player and make our family proud."

He went out and hired a harp teacher and bought a lovely little harp for his son.

Every day the boy took his harp to the teacher for a lesson. He wanted to learn, but he wasn't very good. His fingers were thick, and hard as he would try, he couldn't play delicately and he continually broke the strings.

The father bought more and stronger strings, but it didn't make any difference. The teacher worked patiently with the boy, but Maung Pon couldn't treat the harp with any sensitivity. Strings kept breaking.

The teacher gave up hope, but the father kept paying for lessons, so the teacher kept working with the boy.

Maung Pon grew into a man. He married and had seven children. His old harp teacher died. The father found a new teacher.

Then the father died. Maung Pon's mother kept paying for lessons and for new harp strings. After she died, Maung Pon paid for his own lessons and strings.

As Maung Pon got older, his teachers were all much younger than he. He bought a lot of different harps, hoping to find one that could stand up to his punishing style of play.

Finally, Maung Pon died. All his harps were stored in the houses of his children and grandchildren. He was forgotten.

Decades later, one of his great grandchildren found an old dusty harp in the back of a closet. He asked other family members where it had come from.

Someone said: "Well, I think I remember we had an ancestor years ago who played the harp. Who was it? Let's see . . . Maung Pon, I think. I seem to recall that he was really good on the harp."

Curious, they asked other relatives, who looked in their closets and storage places. Many of the old harps turned up. The relatives talked more and more about Maung Pon, and exchanged stories about his beautiful and tender playing. There was some disagreement about certain details, but over time all the stories coalesced. The family spoke with pride of their talented ancestor.

Thus it was, after almost one hundred years, Maung Pon fulfilled his father's hopes.

Now, you might be thinking that this story is about

the stupidity of staying with something long after it's clear that it's a lost cause. What does Kenny Rogers say in that country song about knowin' when to hold 'em and knowin' when to fold 'em?

But the story can also be about defining success differently. In our culture, we want, expect success right away. This story gives success another context.

It illuminates Bejamin Disraeli's quotation: "The secret of success is consistency of purpose."

Whether you
succeed or not is
irrelevant—there is
no such thing.
Making your
unknown known is
the important
thing—and keeping
the unknown
always beyond you.

—Georgia O'Keeffe, in a letter
to Sherwood Anderson, 1923

Everyman takes the limits of his own
field of vision for the limits of the world.

—Arthur Schopenhauer

Do not shorten
the morning by
getting up late;
look upon it as
quintessence of
life, as to a
certain extent
sacred.

—Arthur
Schopenhauer

22: CREATIVITY

Write It Down

Ira Progoff died in 1998. He was a psychotherapist and author. Progoff's major contribution was journaling, as he called it. He taught workshops to over 200,000 people in keeping intensive personal journals.

He believed that through journaling, people could focus on the spiritual and creative potentials of their lives.

Julia Cameron, author of *The Artist's Way*, recommends morning pages, writing three pages in a journal every morning as a way to reconnect with our artist within. Cameron's morning pages are rooted in Progoff's theories.

I wrote morning pages for a year. Some of the time, I used them to air my gripes and complaints about how unfair life was. I found it cleared the air around me. I felt lighter and happier the rest of the day—I had jettisoned the dead weight of my stuff.

In the book, *The Einstein Factor,* by Win Wenger and Richard Poe, the authors write:

> In the 1920s, researcher Catherine Cox studied 300 geniuses from history, such as Sir Isaac Newton, Thomas Jefferson, and Johann Sebastian Bach. . . .
>
> One sign of genius, Cox noted, was a

penchant for . . . recording thoughts and feelings in diaries, poems, and letters to friends and family, starting from an early age. Cox observed this tendency not only in budding writers, but in generals, statesmen, and scientists.

It has been estimated that fewer than one percent of the population habitually engage in writing out their thoughts, experiences, and perceptions, whether in journals, diaries, letters, or books. But, with startling consistency, the world's top achievers seem to fall in that critical 1 percent. . . .

[W]as the scribbling, in and of itself, a mechanism by which people who were not born geniuses unconsciously nurtured and activated a superior intellect?

Progoff wrote, "Each human life has the potentiality of becoming an art work."

Any of us who keep a journal, for whatever reason, owes a debt to Progoff for helping to bring the concept into the mainstream.

But, we may say, we don't have time to keep a journal. We're too busy. As in, we don't have time to nurture our creativity to become better problem solvers.

The old Zen monk would smile and say, "Is that so."

You don't have to spend a lot of time writing to get a payoff. For example, in *The Einstein Factor*, Wenger and Poe describe what they call "The Portable Memory Bank Technique":

You buy a small notebook and carry it around with you wherever you go, just as young Einstein and Faraday did. Write down in that notebook any stray thoughts that come into your head, whether or not they seem worth recording at the time.

The technique works because of the First Law of Behavioral Psychology. Whenever you write down a perception or an idea, you reinforce the behavior of being perceptive or creative. Whenever you fail to describe or record such insights, you reinforce the behavior of being unperceptive and uncreative.

You will not have to practice this technique long before you notice a sharp increase in the number and quality of creative thoughts that pop into your head.

I've got my notebook in my pocket. Try it yourself.

What do you plan to do with
your one wild and precious life?

—Mary Oliver

23: QUOTATIONS

The Axe for the Frozen Sea Inside Us

I was driving in my car, listening to a tape called "Simple Abundance," by Sarah Ban Breathnach. I was sort of half-listening, you know, daydreaming a bit (not being present!), when I heard this line: "Not all hours are billable."

I drove on, the tape played on, but that line stuck with me. It seemed oddly profound. "Not all hours are billable."

To you, it may seem more mundane and obvious than profound, so let me explain. After I'd had my own business for a few years, I was in deep financial trouble. I hired June Anderson, a business coach, to help me turn it around. Because my business practices were so poor at first, she really held my feet to the fire about not wasting time. Though she never used the term "billable hours," I was drilled over and over in the concept to the point where if I did any reading to research a topic, I felt guilty that it wasn't forwarding my business in a more direct way.

June's not my coach any more, but a strong habit was put into place. The quotation felt like the loosening of a tight belt.

My point isn't about the quotation itself, it's about how it struck me so forcefully. That's what we want quotations to do, to slam us between the eyes and wake us up to some truth, to act as a beacon, drawing us out of ourselves, energizing us.

Franz Kafka said it so much better when he described books we should read:

> I think we ought to read only the kind of books that wound and stab us. . . . We need the books that affect us like a disaster, that grieve us deeply, like the death of someone we loved more than ourselves, like being banished into forests far from everyone, like a suicide. A book must be the axe for the frozen sea inside us.

What quote has been the axe for the frozen sea inside you lately? Have you put it up where you can see it often? Do you share it with others? Has it been a while since one has "wounded and stabbed" you? Be on the lookout. It's out there, waiting for you.

24: SUMMING IT ALL UP

"The Precious Jewel"
A Sufi Tale

Once upon a time, in a far away place of beauty and peace, there dwelt a just king and queen. They had two beautiful children, a son and a daughter. Life was good.

When the children were entering adolescence, their father brought them together and said:

"It is time for you both to go on a long journey to a faraway land. I want you to find a precious Jewel and return with it. It will not be easy. Take care, and watch out for one another."

The brother and sister were given disguises and escorted to a very strange land. Fog was everywhere and it never went away. The citizens of this dark place moved slowly past each other, feeling their way through the gloom. The fog started to affect the two travellers. They began to feel as though they were sleepwalking.

Every once in a while they would catch a glimpse of something, some shadow, that reminded them of their home. Sometimes they thought they saw the Jewel, but they began to think of the dark land as real, and they wandered away from each other and were lost.

The king heard of their predicament and sent a

wise old man to help them.

The old man reunited them and told them, "Wake up, remember your goal, and stay together."

His words awakened them. With the help of the wise old man they faced the terrible obstacles surrounding the Jewel.

When they finally possessed it, they used its power to return to their own realm where there was no fog and only light.

And they lived in happiness for evermore.

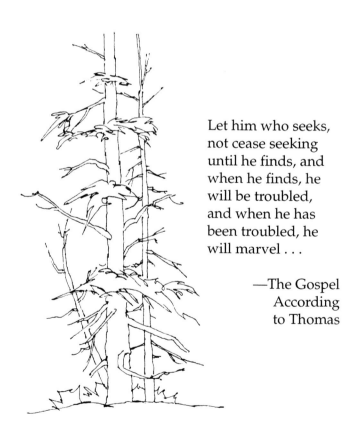

Let him who seeks, not cease seeking until he finds, and when he finds, he will be troubled, and when he has been troubled, he will marvel . . .

—The Gospel According to Thomas

AFTERWORD

A man approached the Buddha.
"I have heard of you," the man said. "Are you a god?"
"No," the Buddha said.
"Are you an angel?"
"No."
"Are you a spirit?"
"No."
"Well, then, what are you?"
The Buddha replied, "I am awake."

REFERENCES

Chapter 2

Redford B. Williams, M.D., and Virginia Williams, Ph.D., *Anger Kills*, Harper Perennial, New York, 1994.

William C. Menninger, M.D., "The Criteria of Emotional Maturity," North Carolina Association for Pastoral Counselors, avaliable from http://www.ncapc.org/pages/maturity.html, Internet, accessed February 28, 2000.

Brad Blanton, Ph.D., *Radical Honesty: How to Transform Your Life by Telling the Truth*, Dell Publishing, New York, 1996.

Christina Feldman and Jack Kornfield, ed., "Samurai and Monk," *Stories of the Spirit, Stories of the Heart*, Harper, San Francisco, 1991, p. 295.

Chapter 3

Christina Feldman and Jack Kornfield, ed., "Zen Monk," *Stories of the Spirit, Stories of the Heart*, Harper, San Francisco, 1991, p. 390.

Chapter 4

Æsop,"The Frogs Asking For A King," *Æsop's Fables*, V.S. Vernon Jones, trans., Avenel Books, New York, 1912.

Chapter 5

Richard Schickle, "Art Was His Fragile Fortress: Stanley Kubrick 1928-1999," Time Magazine ,March 22, 1999.

Thaddeus Golas, *The Lazy Man's Guide to Enlightenment*, The Seed Center, Palo Alto, CA, 1971.

Chapter 10

Sam Keene, *Faces of the Enemy*, Harper & Row, 1986.

Chapter 11

John Hatt, *The Tropical Traveler*, Hyppocrene Books, Inc., New York, 1985.

Chapter 12

T.S. Eliot, "The Love Song of J. Alfred Prufrock," *Collected Poems 1909-1962*, Harcourt Brace & Company, San Diego, CA.

Erica Goode, "New Study Finds Middle Age Is Prime of Life," *New York Times*, February 16, 1999.

Chapter 15

Christina Feldman and Jack Kornfield, ed., "Two Monks and a Woman At a Puddle," *Stories of the Spirit, Stories of the Heart*, Harper, San Francisco, pp. 199, 346.

Chapter 16

Rabbi Zuzya quote, Martin Burber, *Tales of Hasidim: The Early Masters*, Schocken Books, New York, 1947, p. 251.

Chapter 21

Harold Courlander, *Tiger's Whiskers and Other Tales from Asia and the Pacific*, 1st Owlet edition, Henry Holt & Company, Inc., New York, September 1995.

Chapter 22

Julia Cameron, *The Artist's Way*, Penguin Putnam, New York, 1992.

Chapter 24

Idries Shah, *Thinkers of the East*, Octagon Press, 1971.

Afterword

Christina Feldman and Jack Kornfield, ed., "What Are You?," *Stories of the Spirit, Stories of the Heart*, Harper, San Francisco, 1991, p. 392.

Give the gift of coping in a chaotic world to your friends, family, and associates— order additional copies of this book directly from Fish Tales Press.

Fax Orders: (408) 998-1742. Send this form.

Telephone Orders: Call toll free 1-877-88DRFISH (1-877-883-7347). Please have your credit card ready.

E-mail Orders: Send your order to RobertFish@aol.com

Postal Orders: Fish Tales Press, 1440 Newport Avenue, San Jose, CA 95125-3329.

Please send _____ book(s) at $14.00 each $_____

Add 8.25% sales tax for orders shipped
to California ($1.16 for each book). $_____

Add $4.00 for shipping and handling
for the first book and $1.00 for each
additional book. $_____

Total: $_____

Payment: ☐ Check or Money Order
              (Please make payable to Robert Fish)

         ☐ Credit Card
              ☐ Visa   ☐ Mastercard
              ☐ AMEX

Card Number: _____

Expiration Date: _____

Signature: _____

Give the gift of coping in a chaotic world to your friends, family, and associates— order additional copies of this book directly from Fish Tales Press.

Fax Orders: (408) 998-1742. Send this form.

Telephone Orders: Call toll free 1-877-88DRFISH (1-877-883-7347). Please have your credit card ready.

E-mail Orders: Send your order to RobertFish@aol.com

Postal Orders: Fish Tales Press, 1440 Newport Avenue, San Jose, CA 95125-3329.

Please send _____ book(s) at $14.00 each $_____

Add 8.25% sales tax for orders shipped to California ($1.16 for each book). $_____

Add $4.00 for shipping and handling for the first book and $1.00 for each additional book. $_____

Total: $_____

Payment: ☐ Check or Money Order
(Please make payable to Robert Fish)

☐ Credit Card
☐ Visa   ☐ Mastercard
☐ AMEX

Card Number: _____

Expiration Date: _____

Signature: _____